PODVIG

FATHER SPYRIDON BAILEY

Also by Father Spyridon:

Journey To Mount Athos
The Ancient Path
Trampling Down Death By Death
Fire On The Lips

PODVIG

FATHER SPYRIDON BAILEY

FaR

Published in 2016 by FeedARead.com Publishing.
Funded by the Arts Council of Great Britain.

Podvig (Russian): a spiritual struggle which draws one closer to Christ.

Chapter 1

War was a rumour that never came near. It was no more than thunder beyond the mountains or a look of fear in the eyes of the weak. For men who had never taken up arms war was forgotten beneath the every-day demands of real life and only existed now in the bitter memories of old men. Young men laughed when they were reminded to be ready though the absence of battle did not bring them real peace: there was always the struggle to pay taxes on time and make plans for the future.

Kellan called the mule to a halt and crouched low to the stretch of ground he had been ploughing. He squeezed a fist of dirt and shook his head at the dry earth. Even in his short life he had seen the rich black soil transformed into this lifeless dust into which men now poured their sweat for so little reward. It was as though the earth itself had grown tired of giving; man's unrelenting demands for harvest had drained its capacity for life. Kellan looked back at the ground he had turned and felt an overwhelming sense of defeat. No matter how hard he struggled he knew he could not force the crops to grow where the earth had been enslaved to the point of infertility.

He looked up at the cloudless sky and tried to pray, but the words appeared on his lips and floated away; his heart was as dead as the soil beneath him. He pulled the mule back across the field and slumped down on a large rock to rest in the shade.

He didn't own the land or the beast he worked with, and rubbing his hands over his face he questioned his reasons for even being there. He felt no connection with the place; his hours of work were for a wage and nothing more, and seeing this forced him to acknowledge a vast emptiness within himself. But recognising this made no difference, he knew there was no other option for men like him and unless he could learn to enjoy the moments of pleasure that life occasionally provided there was little else to hope for in the countless days that stretched out before him. Realising this only made him angry; he resented his lot and had a vague sense that someone must be to blame. He thought about the other fields that were allotted to the boss's friends, and the strong healthy animals that were appointed to work them. The injustice made him bitter and he wasn't prepared to work hard when he was treated so unfairly. It wasn't just what other people did to him; he sensed that the world and life itself had somehow plotted against him.

He sat motionless for over an hour, not caring if anyone found him not doing his work. It was only mid-afternoon but he knew he couldn't face going back to ploughing the field; the futility of the task had drained him of even being able to go through the motions for the sake of a pay packet. Eventually the mule grew restless and so Kellan headed back towards town, trying to think of how he could explain his early return. With about half a mile to go he raised his gaze from the ground before him and saw columns of smoke rising from the direction of home. He stood still for a moment, confused at what he was seeing and desperately trying to make sense of what it could mean. He yanked at the leather reins around the mule's head and began to trot quickly along the road.

As he grew nearer to town he began to hear screams and the smoke rising into the blue sky had turned thick and dark. Without thinking he let go of the mule and began to run the last section of road, his heart beating a panicked pulse in his chest and head. About a hundred yards before the edge of town came into sight Kellan swerved off the road and climbed a grass bank into a few trees that provided a view of the scene. As he got to the top of the rise he dropped to his belly and crawled to a place where he could see without being seen. To his horror many of the houses were burning and around them was a scene of carnage and brutality. A number of bloodied bodies lay scattered as though they had tried to run but had been caught as they fled and the sound of women's screaming let him know the horror of what was taking place.

Kellan pulled back out of sight and lay motionless beneath one of the trees; his body shook with a fear that paralysed him even as he listened to the screams for help. His only impulse was of self-preservation, he slowly crawled back down the bank and once he was back at the road he began to run. The mule was startled as he approached but Kellan was oblivious to it, he raced past and on along the road, every step promising safety and escape. He ran on long after his lungs were burning for oxygen, the terror driving him beyond his normal capacities. Eventually he had no choice but to stop and lurched into the concealment of some bushes where he fell to the ground and gasped for air. As he lay there he strained to hear every possible sound around him, afraid that someone had seen and pursued him. But beyond his own laboured breathing he heard nothing, not even the cries from town. With a dense covering of branches over him he began to feel safe and decided to hide until night fall. He curled into a tight ball, still listening for any sign of approaching danger. He even dared to close his eyes, his mind now filled with every sound his ears detected.

The hours passed slowly and through the leaves he could see the sky growing dark. But even now he was too afraid to risk coming out of hiding and for the rest of the night he lay drifting in and out of shallow sleep. He woke the following morning and was disorientated by his surroundings until the memory of the previous day suddenly struck him and he was thrown back into the reality of what had happened. For a short while he listened carefully in order to convince himself that he really was alone. Once he was sure there was nothing to hear he slowly pushed his head out from the covering and searched the road in both directions for any sign of life. Everything was still and he carefully pulled himself to his feet. He looked at the road that headed away from town and his instinct was to quickly put as much distance between himself and any possible danger. But he looked back from where he had run and knew he had to see what had happened. He paused momentarily to overcome the desire to get away and began walking back towards town. It was not an impulse to rescue anyone in need, only a need to know what had happened.

As he walked his eyes scanned the hills around him, he was alert to every movement of branch and flower in the wind and several times he stopped to listen for any approaching threat. Gradually he made his way back to where he had climbed the bank to look down on the town and carefully he repeated his slide into position. There was some smoke rising from where fires still smouldered but most had now burned out. Once more he crawled to the very edge of the bank and stared in disbelief at the destruction before him. Most of the houses were gutted; the charred structures looked disfigured and ugly, their black beams still framing the shapes where lives had been lived. Other than the little smoke still rising nothing moved, the town was dead. But Kellan still stayed in position for a while to convince himself that there was no one about, and only when he was satisfied that he was alone did he tentatively move down the bank towards the first of the buildings.

He immediately noticed that the bodies he had seen the day before had been removed, there was no obvious sign that human beings had once been here. Nothing of the buildings had been left untouched, even sheds and barns had been hacked and burned. Kellan sensed a fury in the desolation, as though the attackers had unleashed hatred in their violence that had driven them to defile everything around them. Kellan made his way to his own home where he knew his sister had been. When he thought about the screams he had heard he was overcome with shame at having run away and was relieved that there were no corpses left to accuse him further. He couldn't bring himself to imagine their fate.

His house was now a mere shell, a roofless set of walls that were blackened by fire. He stepped over the remains of the front door and realised that many things had been taken before the house was burned. As he stood in the middle of what had been their kitchen he began for the first time to weep. He pressed his face into his hands as though to conceal his emotions but his chest shook as he sobbed. He made his way into his bedroom and found a single blanket under the remains of his bed. He rolled it up and threw it over his shoulder as he looked around for anything more he could salvage. But there was nothing and he couldn't stand to be there any longer. He went back out into the street and looked around at his neighbours' homes. He considered searching them for anything that might be of use to him but couldn't bring himself to go in. They had been violated enough without him looting their last possessions.

He found a leather water bottle next to a pump and filled it with water. He took a swig and felt a sting on his dry lips that had cracked in the sun. He topped up the bottle and threw the strap across his shoulder to hold the blanket in place.

In a state of confusion and fear he made his way back out through the town hardly able to take in the reality of what was around him. He tried to tell himself that if he had come back he would now be dead, that whoever had done this was clearly capable of dealing with him, that he couldn't have been of help to anyone, not even his sister; but his shame only deepened. He climbed the grass bank and sat staring at the remains of the town, unsure of what to do next. He knew there was no point in staying but he couldn't think of where else to go. Walking away didn't seem right, abandoning the place seemed to deny what had happened and he felt an irrational need to remain as a witness to the people who had gone. But he knew no one would come to hear his story, and in truth he could never bring himself to tell all of it. The smell of soot filled his nostrils and added to his sense of sickness. As he took in the scene he found his fear being replaced with a terrible realisation: he no longer cared if he lived or died. Life had seemed pointless enough already, but now the ideas of courage and virtue that he had liked to play with were gone: in the face of danger he had run. Just as the town had been destroyed so the illusion he had carried about who and what he was had crumbled. He was left with nothing, within or without. While others had died, no doubt bravely trying to defend those they loved, he had saved his own skin before all else, and in his shame he now continued to live. But it was life without value, the life of a coward;

he understood that self-preservation was meaningless if there is nothing to live for.

He had come to no conclusion about where he would go but mechanically he got to his feet and began to walk away. He no longer looked around him; his gaze was fixed at the ground ahead. Even his tears had now dried up, and as he slowly plodded along the road he knew no physical distance would be enough to separate him from the effects of what had happened. It was still early morning but he didn't look to see where the sun was for time or direction. As the hours passed his slow but steady pace moved him on away from familiar roads until the world around him was unknown. But whereas once he would have felt lost now he had no desire to belong or be reassured by home. One place was the same as the next; in his numbness he was only aware of the pads of his feet moving him on along the road.

Eventually thirst forced him to a halt and he glanced around at the unfamiliar open fields that surrounded him. A brief moment of fear cut through him once more when he realised how exposed he was in such flat country and he looked to the horizons for somewhere to conceal himself and rest. In the distance to the east was the dense covering of a forest to which he now headed. He clambered over dry stone walls and low fences as he crossed fields, quickening his pace now that he was out in the open for fear of being spotted. His hands became grazed and bloodied from climbing hedges but eventually the forest was near. He came to a halt and stood staring at the dark green foliage and the deep shadows beneath the trees. As a child he had always be warned about entering forests alone and old ladies had told stories about bears eating the unwary. He remembered his grandmother and was bitterly relieved that she had not lived long enough to witness these days. The face of his grandfather appeared before him and he shuddered once more at what had happened.

Feeling the immediate coolness as he stepped out from beneath the sun Kellan entered the forest. There was little space between the trees and low branches and undergrowth made movement difficult. But eventually he found a narrow path worn into the forest floor by some unknown animal and instinctively he began following where ever it took him.

Chapter 2

Even on a hot, windless day the canopy above him seemed to swirl in a constant rustle of movement as the high air currents passed through the leaves. Kellan's attention however, remained fixed to the ground as he picked his way along the animal path. The edge of the forest was now long gone and without sight of the sky it was impossible to know which way he was heading. The little light that cut through the foliage was beginning to dim and the approach of evening began to panic him. The great height of the trees above him made him feel vulnerable even while he was confident no one would find him here. As the light began to fade he could no longer be sure he was following the animal track and it became increasingly difficult to force his way through the thick brambles. Eventually he grew tired of making the effort and knowing it would be impossible to find his way out in the dark, he decided to find a place to lie down. He noticed a small patch of grass beneath a fallen tree and wrapping his blanket tightly around him he pressed his body deep into what he hoped would be a place of concealment.

Darkness came quickly and with it the sounds of animals moving through the under growth. He knew they would have all been aware of him crashing through the forest, and he imagined them in the dark picking up his scent and moving towards him. He began to wish he'd thought of breaking off a length of stick to protect himself but now it was too late and he pulled tighter at the blanket for security. Eventually he drifted off into a fitful sleep, waking every thirty minutes or so as his back and limbs tightened and complained at the uneven ground and biting cold. Each time he woke he found himself once again in an alien world with no hope of home offering reassurance.

Morning caught him dreaming. As he slipped into waking consciousness he could still hear the voices of friends as they chatted in a now non-existent reality. Even before the physical world around him made any impact the memory of those voices wrenched at his psyche, everything he had ever known was gone. The same dull ache returned to his chest as he began to become aware of his physical senses. Everything was wet with dew; it had penetrated his blanket making his clothes feel cold and heavy. The air was crisp and damp as it hung around the huge trees that stretched up above him. The discordant caw of a crow gave voice to the forest's displeasure at his intrusion but he was beyond caring whether or not the world wanted his presence.

He sat up and found his water bottle. Lifting it above his head he squeezed the last few drops onto his tongue and knew that it wasn't enough to quench his thirst. He leaned his face into the bush next to him and feeling like a dog he licked the moisture from the leaves. It brought a little relief but dehydration was prompting his physical system to seek more. As he stood he looked around for signs of a path or anything that might indicate the best direction to follow. All around him the same thick bush filled the gaps between the trunks of trees. The forest hadn't seemed so large from outside but now from within he understood its depths. He had no choice but to start moving but he knew it would be good fortune alone that would bring him to an exit. Looking up at the shafts of light that reached down to the forest floor he decided to try and find a break in the canopy that would allow him to judge the position of the sun. He hoped this might provide the opportunity to get his bearings enough to work out which way to head, but he knew he was no expert in such things.

Walking was difficult and to avoid tripping his attention remained on the ground. Every so often he stopped to search for daylight but the ceiling of thick darkness remained unbroken. Thirst gripped his throat and a number of times he put the empty bottle to his mouth in the hope of finding a final drop that he might have missed. He strained to hear running water and twice the rustle of leaves gave him false hope. As the hours passed he grew weaker as the thought of dying alone here grew stronger.

He sat to rest on a fallen tree and watched countless insects scurrying in and out of the rotting wood. He shuddered at the prospect of eventually lying down on the forest floor and the same fate befalling him. The thought of his rotting corpse attracting other animals was too much to bear, it was somehow worse than death itself, and he let out a weak sob. But there were no tears; it was a dry, hopeless act of fear and self-pity.

As he struggled with his situation a new threat revealed itself. From somewhere unseen he heard the loud breath of an animal; it exhaled from a large chest in a deep, confident snort. Kellan froze in fear and expectation of the animal's attack, but it came no closer. After a few minutes he heard the crash of undergrowth as it moved away but he remained still, wanting to be sure it was far away before he made any sound. As he stood he looked around for signs of danger but could see nothing. He slowly began to walk away from the direction of the noise, looking now as much to the rear to spot anything in pursuit as he did to find a path.

His hands were now shaking from lack of water and he couldn't focus his thoughts clearly. Without realising how long he had been on the move he caught sight of the sky but his heart sank to realise that it was coloured with evening. Soon the little light he had would leave him and in his weakened state he knew he was vulnerable to anything that might be interested in him. He half-collapsed to the ground and pulled his arms around his head as if to hide from everything. The fantasy of finding his way out had left him and he knew he would die if he did not find water.

The same snorting from earlier now startled him and he stared into the shadows, wondering what shape was about to lurch towards him. He braced himself for the attack and then watched as a huge animal slowly stepped into view. It was a mature stag, its antlers spread menacingly above its powerful neck and shoulders. Kellan looked into its dark eyes and despite his fear was overcome with relief at the sight of another living being. The deer bowed its head slightly and repeatedly scraped the ground with its foot, as though preparing to charge. But then as though dismissing the fool who had wandered into its territory, it snorted once more before turning and slowly wandered away without any concern for Kellan's presence and with an air of complete self-assurance.

Kellan considered trying to follow the creature in the hope of being led to water but knew he could never keep up. Besides, he couldn't be sure he wouldn't provoke it into violence and accepted that he was once more alone. Without even glancing at the ground behind him he lay back, his blanket still tied in a tight roll beside him. He looked up at the trees and felt the solid earth beneath him. The whole world was moving through space with his tiny form clinging pointlessly to its surface without reason or purpose, and now he was going to die. Without humour he recognised the irony of having run from danger to save himself only now to throw away his life through stupidity. What had he gained from these extra hours of life? The futility of his cowardly impulse was overwhelming and in a state of exhaustion and complete dehydration he fell into a sleep that was less than sleep, devoid of rest or dreams.

Chapter 3

A damp cloth touched his lips and though it brought a sharp sting Kellan instinctively sucked some of the moisture into his mouth. His eyes were reluctant to open but through slits he could make out a figure bending over him. The cloth returned with more water and again Kellan gratefully took what was given. As his vision regained its focus he could make out an old face framed in long grey hair and a straggly beard. As he looked up he met the gaze of eyes full of pity and then he lost consciousness once more.

It was impossible for him to tell how long he had been lying there but as Kellan began to stir he could feel the warmth of a blanket folded over him and the absence of any real chill in the air that immediately told him he was indoors. He didn't have the strength to raise his head but turned a little to find out where he was. The room was dark except for a soft yellow glow that emanated from the small flame of an oil lamp that hung from the far wall. In the halo of light Kellan could make out a painting in subdued colours but he couldn't identify the detail. His chest tightened as he coughed and from the shadows before the painting a figure turned towards him. Dressed in black and completely motionless he had been invisible in the half light but as he crossed in front of the lamp the outline of a small man came into view. He moved off out of sight for a moment and without saying anything brought the moist cloth back to Kellan's lips.

Kellan nodded in response and took the cloth and held it against his face. The cool relief eased a little of his discomfort but then he was overcome with a coughing fit that seemed to rip at his abdomen. When it subsided the figure reappeared and once more provided a newly dampened cloth. The care being shown to him reassured Kellan and without any anxiety he closed his eyes to rest and quickly fell back into sleep.

The next time he woke he felt a little stronger and managed to raise himself to his elbows. The room was small and bare except for a metal stove in one corner from which a thin chimney snaked up and out through the roof. Other than this there were no clues as to whether he was in a cave or a man-made structure, but the regularity and smoothness of the walls was evidence of someone having worked hard on the space even if they hadn't created it.

As he glanced around he realised that once more he had failed to notice the figure of the old man who this time was bent over on the floor before the oil lamp. Kellan couldn't be sure if the man was sleeping but then detected a low voice that was repeating phrases in a calm, unhurried manner that was clearly the sound of someone in prayer. Kellan lay back and tried to make out the words but couldn't quite hear them. But the voice was calm and the tone relaxed him a little. He closed his eyes and almost began to feel at ease when suddenly he remembered being in the forest and what had taken him there. The memory of the fate of his village immediately clutched at his heart and he let out an involuntary groan.

The figure on the ground raised him self and slowly came to Kellan's side. His face was now much clearer and Kellan realised that the man who had been caring for him was of a great age. His hair and beard were not just grey but pure white, and though the man's face was full of compassion he still said nothing.

"Where am I?" Kellan's voice was weak and rasped with dehydration.

"You are safe, try to relax a little."

"How long have I been here?" Kellan needed to locate himself at least in time even if his physical location was a mystery.

"Nearly three days now," the man's voice was gentle but firm. "You are looking a little stronger."

"Three days!" Kellan could hardly believe it. The old man smiled but said nothing more.

"How did I get here?"

"I found you not far from my cell," the old man replied. "I thought I had come across a corpse. I don't know how long you'd been there but a few more hours and I think I would have had to bury you." Kellan was a little shocked at his bluntness and watched as the old man turned and disappeared into the shadows for a moment, only to return with a small wooden bowl.

"You should eat, but just a little; it will help you regain your strength."

Kellan managed to sit up and rest his back against the wall behind him.

"I'm Kellan, what is your name?"

"Father Paisios."

"A priest?"

"No," replied the old man, "just a simple monk." He lifted the bowl once more to encourage Kellan to eat. It contained a small portion of vegetables that had been boiled soft and needed little chewing. Kellan gratefully spooned a little into his mouth as the old man stood watching.

"Thank you," said Kellan, "for the food and for bringing me here."

The man chuckled a little, "What was I going to do, let you rot out in the forest?" He took the bowl and walked over to where a wooden bucket sat near the stove. Kellan looked around to take in more of the room. He could now see a door in the opposite wall but there were no windows. A single box that could also be used as a seat was the only piece of furniture in what looked a very basic existence. Father Paisios occupied himself with cleaning the bowl as though he was alone but Kellan was keen to talk.

"Where exactly are we?" .

"We are very close to where I found you sleeping, another ten minutes of walking and you might have found my cell."

Kellan resented the suggestion that he had been sleeping in the forest, it seemed to underplay what he had been through, but he let it go. "Are we safe from bandits?"

The old man turned and looked at him for a moment, a thoughtful tightening of his brow suggested he was giving the question some thought. "You will not be bothered by them here."

"Are they afraid to enter the forest?" Kellan asked, a little frustrated with the answer.

"No, they will attack people where ever they go, but you needn't worry yourself, you are safe."

Kellan realised that once more his mind was preoccupied with his own wellbeing, the same thoughts that had led him to run when the village was attacked. Even now he was a coward, looking to an old man for reassurance: but as repulsed as he was at all these things in himself he couldn't overcome them. The vague reassurances the old man had given did help, but it wasn't a conscious choice Kellan was making, something deep within him was driven by fear.

Seeming to perceive his visitor's feelings the old man said "Not one hair of your head is unknown to God. You must believe that you are in his care. Even when you experience sorrows you must know that as long as you are faithful and obedient, all that happens to you is God's will."

Kellan was surprised at how forthright Father Paisios was speaking to him, but despite his lack of care for such matters the statement struck him deeply.

"How can I believe that God would want all of this for me?" Kellan spat contemptuously.

"God's love for you is infinitely greater than your own love for yourself, when we know this we are able to accept all that comes to us." The old man's voice was steady and firm.

"How can that be? You don't know what's happened...or what I've done." Kellan's voice trembled with emotion.

"Our thoughts are not God's thoughts; we cannot reach up and pull down to earth the infinite mind of God. Our thoughts are driven by desire and fear; His thoughts are concerned only with our salvation. We cannot see as God sees, this is why we become so obsessed with worldly concerns and with our own physical wellbeing. Only when we abandon such distractions and give ourselves to His infinite love and care do we find any kind of peace."

Kellan shook his head, "How can we wait for death to know peace?"

"This peace can be known even in this world," the old man drew nearer. "Always remember that God loves us more than the devil hates us."

Kellan was struck by this and wondered why the old man had said such a thing. He looked intently at the wrinkled face before him and saw Father Paisios' expression break into a smile.

"You must trust that you are safe here, I will tend to your physical needs while you are recovering...and God will heal your heart."

Kellan wanted to ask more but fell silent; there was something about the monk that unsettled him. He lay back and felt grief engulf him once more; there could be no relief even for a moment. The old man returned to standing before the oil lamp and Kellan detected the rhythm of his prayers as they

26

began again. The food had given him a little energy and the comfort of a full belly eased his mood a little. He closed his eyes and once more fell to sleep.

Another day of sleep and waking for short periods passed before Kellan finally woke and knew that he had returned to a state nearing normality. Father Paisios had fed him a number of times and Kellan's body had begun to regain its strength. Sitting up he swung his legs over the side of the makeshift bed and realised he was alone. The sense of returning strength emboldened him to know more about the monk and though still a little shaky on his feet he walked over to the painting that was illuminated by the oil lamp. He now recognised the image as the Mother of God. Her eyes were full of pity and Kellan understood something of her pain as she held her son who was to suffer. More than Christ's sufferings Kellan felt a connection with the one who mourned for her child, and without knowing how or why, he felt she could help him with his own grief. But it was as though his hands were tied, he didn't know how to reach out to her, and a little surprised at his own reaction to the painting he turned away.

From his new perspective he realised that the room was a wooden construction with walls of smoothed earth. He stooped down to the bucket and lifted himself a cup of water. It was fresh and tasted good. He gulped a second and then headed for the door. Though roughly made it was a good fit and he pushed it open without much effort.

The world outside was bathed in the smells and sounds of early morning. There were many more birds singing than he remembered hearing as he had walked through the forest and above him a break in the canopy allowed shafts of warm light to pour down on and around the little hut. Kellan turned to examine the structure. It was a low building, barely taller than an average man, its sloping roof was covered in branches arranged carefully to keep it water proof. Being so small and tucked away between two thick-trunked trees it would be easily missed by anyone passing by and Kellan suspected he would never have seen it even if he had managed to stumble on a little further.

He looked around for signs of the old man but there was nothing to indicate where he might be. Even with the assurance of the hut Kellan was a little nervous to be alone and hoped his host would return soon. He found a stump that was worn smooth from being used as a seat and rested himself there. He raised his face up to meet the sun's rays and the heat felt good on his skin. He closed his eyes and tried to still his thoughts, but within him the turmoil continued to swirl. As he sat like this the unmistakeable sound of the stag moving through the branches quite near startled Kellan and he watched for signs of the animal. It was like this that Father Paisios returned to find him and seeing Kellan's frightened expression he let out his now familiar chuckle. Kellan was immediately embarrassed to be caught like this, the presence of another person neutralised his anxiety and his body was released from its tension leaving him feeling foolish.

"I heard an animal," he explained, "I think it was a stag. I saw it as I came here."

"Oh yes," smiled Father Paisios, "he is a large fellow, but he won't harm you."

"How can you know that? I have heard stories about people being attacked."

"Why would he want to attack you? You have nothing to fear Kellan."

Losing any need to conceal his feelings Kellan said "I have always been afraid in the forest. Ever since I was a boy. It is full of unknown sounds, and it's so easy to lose your way. How can you live out here like this?"

"The voice of the forest is the comfort God sends to me." Father Paisios sat on another stump as he spoke. "It took me many years to hear this voice speaking, like you I only heard noises for a long time. At first I only heard hunger in the wolf's cry and irritation in the growl of the bear. But slowly God opened my ears, I began to listen to Him speak through the forest, in the wind as it moves through the branches of the trees, telling me of approaching rain, the changing colours signalling the movement of the seasons. In the call of the birds I also hear the forest glorifying God; He is glorified in all things. The heavens and the earth proclaim His glory, but only when our hearts are filled with prayer do we begin to hear the hymn of God's creation. All things sing to Him, all things reveal something of their maker: but only the human heart was blessed to know Him so completely. But as you know, the human heart also has the capacity to know greater loneliness and pain than any other creature: Christ taught us that the kingdom of heaven is within us but too often we spend our time building hell there."

As he paused he smiled gently at Kellan who now stared back at him.

"I hear only threats and danger," he admitted.

"That is because you have not yet begun to listen properly."

"I want to learn how to listen," admitted Kellan.

"Before you can hear God speak you must learn how to pray."

"Can you teach me?"

"Nothing teaches prayer more than prayer itself," said Father Paisios, "you will learn."

Chapter 4

Over the next few days Kellan began to adjust to the pattern of the old man's life. It consisted of long hours before the painting of the Mother of God repeating prayers which Kellan was vaguely familiar with from his childhood. From his wooden box Father Paisios produced two ancient prayer books which Kellan tried to follow as the old man repeated prayers by heart. It was a frustrating process and often Kellan would just stand quietly alongside him, joining in with the Lord's Prayer and other familiar verses. Unless asked direct questions Father Paisios rarely instigated conversation and after an initial uneasiness Kellan adapted to the silence which was slowly changing into something more than an absence of sound.

Kellan had almost completely recovered all of his strength and was keen to make himself useful. Despite his great age Father Paisios was very active outside the hut but Kellan insisted on lifting anything heavy and chopping their wood. Father Paisios never slept in a bed, the brief periods he allowed himself to sleep were spent sitting upright on top of the wooden box. Kellan realised that his own bed had been arranged by Father Paisios as an addition to the usual arrangements of the room and once he was gone it would be taken down.

Kellan found the physical labour a relief from the focussed hours of prayer and through it he was occasionally able to clear his mind of the thoughts that constantly tormented him. The same images repeatedly passed through him, and whatever he tried to think about always led him to the memory of how he had run away from the village. It was like an invisible weight that he could not put down, pressing his soul into submission. He would shake his head violently as if to scramble or dismiss the thoughts, but immediately they would return.

Father Paisios observed this behaviour but said nothing. He didn't offer advice or prompt a strategy for recovery. But Kellan sensed that the old man's prayers were supporting him and even when they were out completing practical tasks he would try to stay close to Father Paisios, feeling a comfort in his physical presence.

One evening they were sitting drinking tea outside the hut; Kellan was in turmoil and in desperation asked "Why am I suffering like this Father?"

The old man paused before answering, he stared at the ground for a moment before his pale eyes looked up and met Kellan's gaze. "Only when we abandon the desire for the pleasures of this world can we ever discover the comfort of God's grace, and only God's grace brings peace in this world."

It wasn't the answer Kellan wanted to hear, he wanted an immediate cure, some thing he could apply to numb his feelings in an instant. Father Paisios sensed how Kellan was thinking and explained "So long as we pursue the joys of this vain world we will endure many miseries in the depths of our hearts. For the ruler of this world attempts to trap us with every form of guile."

"But why?" Kellan asked.

"Out of hatred for us. But God offers love, the love of a true father. If only we have the faith to abandon ourselves to God's mercy we can experience the kingdom of God within us: but so long as we are set on the treasures of the world we plunge ourselves into the darkness of hell."

Kellan shook his head. Not because he rejected Father Paisios' words, but because he felt the cause of his grief was something more than this.

"I do not feel a desire for anything worldly Father, in fact I want nothing."

"Are you sure about that Kellan?"

"Yes Father, quite sure. My grief comes from something else."

"What do you think causes your sorrow?"

Kellan responded without hesitation "I acted as a coward Father, I..." he could barley bring himself to admit what he had done, "I abandoned my village when it was attacked. I ran and thought only of my own safety."

Father Paisios sat looking at him, giving him every chance to add anything more. Eventually he responded with an unexpected question. "Was not your whole life before this a self-serving endeavour?"

Kellan was caught off guard, "What do you mean? I never did anything like this before." There was a little anger in his voice.

"Are you sure?" Father Paisios persisted.

"I don't know what you mean Father, what are you suggesting? My pain is caused by that one moment of cowardice. If I could travel back in time I would gladly lay down my life."

Father Paisios looked down at the ground and shook his head a little. "Wasn't your mind always looking for ways to make things easier for yourself? Why would you expect to suddenly change in that moment when you were threatened with death? We must crucify ourselves daily; deny the flesh its power over us. We must become martyrs every day so that when called to give away our life for God or neighbour it is as though we are giving away nothing. Only when we live for God and not ourselves do we joyfully leap from this world to paradise."

"This is too much for me Father; I am not ready to hear these things. I can think of my cowardice, nothing else means anything to me."

"Are you any less brave than you were a month ago?"

"You know I am," said Kellan, "I have acted like a coward."

"Do you imagine your courage suddenly left you? Of course it didn't, you were no braver then than you are now. The only difference is that a month ago you could pretend to yourself that you were brave: this terrible event simply opened your eyes to the truth of yourself."

Kellan didn't want to believe this but he knew it was true. He half-whispered "What am I?"

"You are a man like any other. But you wanted to pretend that you were more than this. We all live with fantasies about ourselves and it is hard to see the truth. When Christ gave sight to the blind the miracle was a message to all of us who are blind. We are blind to the truth, the full truth of ourselves, the truth of other people and most importantly the truth of God. We live with these fantasies about ourselves so that we can feel we are good and decent. We ignore the truth because it is too painful and makes us ashamed. We ignore the truth of other people and look upon them as cartoons drawn on a page. We do not see the depth of their feelings; we ignore the reality of their pain: how else could we treat one another so badly? But worse than all of this is our blindness to God. We turn away from Him and conjure up for ourselves false ideas or accept the lies of the devil. We all need a miracle, the miracle of God's grace to give us sight."

"I was overcome with fear Father, all I could think of was to cling to life."

"That is because you have not yet died to this world in your heart."

"Why should we want to die in this way Father, it makes no sense to me."

"Do not be afraid to enter your tomb even before the hour of physical death. He who seeks God must abandon everything in this world to which he fastens the grip of his hope. Only when we are accustomed to entering the tomb and embracing death can we lay hold of life that is eternal.

Whenever the devil stirs within us sinful longings we must call to mind the inevitable hour of our death and the judgement that follows it. This is how we strengthen the soul to resist his entrapments."

"But when I remember what I have done I feel nothing but despair and shame."

"This is because you do not have hope in God's mercy," said Father Paisios. "None of us could stand before God if we only had our sins to present before Him: the only proper response is to be ashamed. But God does not abandon us to our sins. He offers forgiveness and healing. If we believe in His infinite love then even our sins may become nothing. We must learn to live in hope of God's love for us: without it there is nothing we can do to be released from the evil we have done."

"But how do I know that God forgives me?"

"Look at this," Father Paisios stood and pointed to the cross above the door of his hut. "Here is God's love for you, do you see it? He did not run away; even to abandon those who hated him. This is our hope."

"What is this hope?" There was now only a genuine desire to understand in Kellan's question.

"It is God's consolation filling the heart. It is a spiritual joy that floods the soul. When God sees our repentance He comes and embraces us. In fleeing the battle you gave yourself as a captive to the enemy and only God can free you. No matter how violently you attack the bars only God can release you from this cage."

Kellan sat silently for a moment, he pressed his head into his hands and rubbed his face.

"But why would God permit such things? Why does He allow us to suffer this way?"

"It is a hard thing to hear Kellan, but suffering is a blessing to us."

"A blessing! How can you say this?"

"Do you not think that God at any moment can crush the demons, chase the devil immediately into the fire? But instead He permits him to beat us a little."

"To what purpose?"

"These beatings shake out the dust from our souls Kellan."

"But why Father? I still don't understand."

"There are many different crowns given in heaven Kellan, the greatest crown is worn by those who willingly suffer for God."

"Father, I don't even know how to begin. You said we must pray, but there must be more. I feel lost. Why should I reject the little comfort I can find in the world?"

"We must seek either worldly consolation or divine consolation, but we must not imagine that we can have both. If we truly want God's consolation we must turn away from every comfort the world has to offer. If we truly die to the pleasures of the world we can know the sweetest delights offered by God. But the devil sets traps for us and in order to avoid them we must struggle with bodily labours: control our food and sleep, give ourselves to constant prayer. If we refuse the fruits of this temporary place we may taste the banquet that is eternal. In order to reach the light of resurrection we must first be crucified."

"What traps Father? I don't yet understand."

Father Paisios' voice remained calm as he spoke. "The devil conceals the truth from us by distorting its nature; this is where our blindness lies."

"But how Father, what does it mean that the devil distorts truth?"

"The devil will make God seem harsh and loveless, encourage us to imagine God is an angry master and all of His commandments given to guide and protect us become cruel, arbitrary and contrary to what feels good. Nowhere is this truer than when it comes to our idea of freedom. The devil will tell you that obedience to God's commands is slavery and that following every worldly impulse or desire is freedom. Of course, the exact opposite is true, so long as we allow our base nature to rule over us our soul is held captive. Freedom can only be found through denial of these cravings, we can only break the chains through fasting and self-denial. Show me the worldly man who thinks he is free and I will reveal the true nature of his freedom by removing the source of his pleasure. Watch as his so-called freedom burns him."

"How do I begin Father, what should my first steps be? I cannot even see peace on the horizon let alone in my soul."

"Let every temptation and trial work for good in your soul. You are afflicted, but in order to be healed we must make these afflictions work for you. Each time you suffer their attacks begin to pray immediately and sorrow will quickly become stepping stones to God. When our thoughts are prompted by weakness or the devil, always let them prompt you to prayer so that even the devil's attacks will work for your salvation. How long do you think the devil will continue to work good? In this way we not only make Satan's attacks work for our salvation but soon the enemy will cease his prompting seeing the good it is doing us."

"I will try Father, thank you."

"Do not think you are the only man to face such trials, but also know that you do not face them alone."

The two men sat finishing their tea as the small patch of sky above them was coloured with approaching evening. Kellan understood that this was only the beginning of his journey but already there was an assurance that touched his heart and he dared to feel hope in the possibility of change. Without explanation Father Paisios stood and as he made his way into the hut he patted Kellan gently on the head. Kellan was surprised at the playfulness of the gesture but grateful for it. He rose and followed the old man into the hut to begin their prayers.

Chapter 5

As days turned into weeks Kellan's outward pattern of life mirrored the routines of Father Paisios in almost every detail. His inner life slowly adapted to the rhythm of prayer and even when he was alone he found himself trying to speak to God. The memories continued to unsettle him but he was no longer struggling alone with them. His awareness of having eaten so much of Father Paisios' food prompted him to work hard when ever he had the opportunity and physical labour proved a consolation. The old man kept a small vegetable patch about half a mile from the hut, situated beneath a large opening in the forest canopy. It constantly amazed Kellan that so much food could be grown under these conditions but Father Paisios would smile and keep repeating "God provides."

One of Kellan's daily tasks was to fetch water from a stream that ran near the garden. A well-worn track led him down to the shallow water where he would carefully collect what was needed. The path had become the route taken by various animals and Kellan was no longer surprised at the sight of rabbits or even deer. Having completed the task so often he returned one day exhausted and dropped the lidless bucket beside the stove.

"Father," he complained, "why didn't you build your cell closer to the stream? What sense does it make to create such needless work?"

The old man looked at him with patience, "I did not choose the location, but I gladly accept the wisdom of it."

"How is it wise Father? And what do you mean you didn't choose it? Did God tell you to settle here?"

The old man smiled at the sarcasm in Kellan's voice. "When I first came to this place I was not alone. I was a young man then, barely twenty; I joined my elder who had been living here for some time."

"Your elder?" Kellan was surprised to hear this. "Who was he Father?"

"My training in monasticism was under the guidance of Father Ephraim, he taught me everything necessary for life here."

"But why would he build his cell so far from the water? Why couldn't he have found a good spot much closer?"

"Because that would have made the water too easy to obtain and we would have been in danger of forgetting its value. Father Ephraim taught me that every drop I bring to the cell is precious; he insisted that we be thankful for every blessing God gives. Think how valuable that pale of water is to you when you wake in the morning or when you return from labour. Do you think you would appreciate its value if the stream was so easily reached?"

"I suppose not Father, but it still feels like you are making life difficult for yourself."

"Difficult?" Father Paisios repeated, "There is no difficulty, only a requirement to work. And this work you complain about brings me into a state of gratitude so surely the task is really a blessing."

Kellan could understand the logic but there was something so ingrained in him that the notion of taking the difficult route was still alien. Father Paisios led him out to the stumps and motioned for him to sit.

"For any tree to bear fruit it must be watered. But if it receives no rain or goats are permitted to chew at its shoots then it will become as lifeless as these stumps. When you carry the water think about what it teaches you."

Kellan sensed his meaning, "Are you talking about prayer?"

"Yes, prayer, and all the ways we receive God's grace."

"Father, I believe that God loves me, so why does He want me to pray?"

"God's grace does not contradict our fee will Kellan; it is the devil who stamps all over our freedom. When we pray for each other God acts in harmony with our free will."

"I am still struggling to pray Father, I have an emptiness inside me that only ever seems to be filled with sorrows."

"We must be careful about the space we create in our hearts," said Father Paisios. "Which voices did you listen to when you were growing up?" Before waiting for an answer he continued "Who did you allow to guide you to this place of emptiness?"

"I'm not sure Father, I didn't really think about it."

"The inner man is like a painter, capturing images of all that he comes into contact with. The soul is like the canvas, where we capture the moral examples we see before us. The soul can be painted with good or evil, it is up to us to seek out holy examples to follow and avoid those who would corrupt us. Unless we actively choose the voices that we allow to guide us we will be pushed and pulled by the vain and proud voices that shout so loud in the world around us. When the heart is young and lacking in wisdom it is vulnerable to the demands of these voices that seem to promise so much. We must learn to think about what it is we are looking for in those who influence us. What do you think impressed you? What outward signs of success did you allow to create the goals you would chase?"

"I understand Father, but that was then. I have been here all these weeks and you have seen how I have tried to pray. What is preventing me from praying like you do?"

"It is not so simple to heal the wounds of a lifetime. Your heart is still so consumed with the things of this world that it has no room for God. You talk about the sense of emptiness within you but the truth is you are filled up with the wrong things. You spent years running far away from Him and then you call out and become confused when you don't hear Him answer. He is gentle with us; He speaks with a still, small voice. In order to hear

43

Him we must still ourselves and draw close to Him. So long as we run aimlessly in every direction the world convinces us that we can never get anywhere. We must learn to shut out the clamour and slowly begin to walk in the direction of home."

"How can we achieve this stillness Father? I'm not even sure I know what it means."

"That is because we spend our lives spinning like a child's toy, bouncing from one worldly desire and impulse to the next. It creates in us the illusion of movement, but in reality we are going nowhere. As we become still we begin to sense the true space around and within ourselves, we see where we are and where we need to go. We must stop running to satisfy our whims and longings, they keep us breathless, running like a puppy after its tail. We must be still Kellan, we must be still."

"But these past weeks you have rarely spoken Father, I have never known such silence. Why hasn't this helped?"

"It will have helped, but this is still a silence that has been enforced upon you, an outer silence that you must allow to enter your heart. Even a monk may sit quietly, not appearing to move, while his mind is in turmoil and his soul is in chaos. Real peace will only grow from inner stillness."

"Father, please teach me to find this inner stillness. It is truly what I desire."

"You have already begun to make the journey, but there is still some distance for you to travel."

"I want to make this journey Father, I know I need to. I can't stay like I am."

"Before we are ready to make the real journey we must leave our home in good order. Before the soul can climb the ladder it must be placed on a firm foundation. It is no good thinking we have climbed many rungs only to discover the feet are sinking."

Father Paisios made the sign of the cross over himself before heading towards the vegetable garden. Kellan silently followed him, allowing the old man's words to find root within him. The old man had a way of walking that seemed effortless and made little sound while Kellan was aware of the noise he made as he pushed through the over-hanging branches. At the garden Father Paisios instructed him to pull out the weeds while he dug out a few potatoes for their meal. Kellan surveyed the soil but could find nothing to remove.

"Father," he insisted, "there aren't any weeds left. You've pulled them all out."

"Keep looking, you'll find some." Father Paisios spoke without turning back to him and remained focussed on his potatoes. Kellan got down on his hands and knees and searched between the vegetables but still couldn't find anything. He began to wonder if the old man was playing a game with him and could feel his frustration rising. Once he had a handful or potatoes Father Paisios stood and looked over at Kellan. Without any difficulty he knelt and pulled up a weed by its roots. He threw it into the undergrowth and then repeated the action with another.

"You don't know what you are looking for Kellan, before you can remove the weeds you must be able to recognise them. A good gardener must know weeds from the crops."

Kellan felt a little foolish and was relieved when after watering the garden Father Paisios announced they should head back to cook their food. As they walked Kellan tried to decipher the incident with the weeds but his embarrassment was still getting in the way.

"Father," he eventually said as they continued to walk, "how do I know what God is saying to me? How can I tell or begin to hear His voice?"

"You must search your heart and find the voice that God has planted within you. Find that small voice of conscience; listen to what it whispers to you. This is how you begin, by listening every day to what that small voice says to you. God placed a holy voice within each of us, one that gently calls us back to purity. We can choose to resist its call, ignore it so that we can no longer even hear it speak to us, or we can pay attention to every word it utters. If we want to hear the voice of God we must begin by hearing and acting on the voice of conscience."

"Are you saying that God's voice is no more than our conscience Father?"

"No, it is much more, but the first step to hearing the holy voice of God is to respond to the holy voice he already placed within us. Only by doing this can we attune ourselves to Him."

"Forgive me if I should not ask this Father, but when you pray do you hear God speaking to you?"

"God speaks to us all, and we are all created to hear Him. Prayer requires that we listen."

"How should I prepare myself for prayer Father?"

"Before we pray we must try to reflect on how we are living and bring to mind our feelings. Only when we have a true sense of our sinfulness and the selfishness that preoccupies us is prayer possible. Only when we recognise the generosity and mercy of God do we enter into a real relationship with Him: without seeing our sinfulness we come before Him as foolish liars unable to receive His grace. True prayer is only possible through God's grace, and we cannot receive it without an awareness of our sins."

"I find it hard Father, I am a proud man and I have always resented when others treat me unfairly."

"You must imitate the grass and soil of the forest Kellan. Even the dumb beasts walk over it and yet still it feeds them and continues to provide for all. Only when we are as humble as the grass will our souls ever know peace. When we see ourselves as the least of all we humbly accept everything with an untroubled mind. The proud man suffers greatly when his good name is insulted but the humble man is crowned by every unjust slander which he accepts with patience."

"I am frightened to think of myself this way Father, I don't know why but I am."

"The proud man raises himself up to the most exalted heights earth can afford, but with every inch he rises he pushes his soul deeper into hell. But the humble man bows low in his poverty while God permits his soul to fly to the heavens."

They reached the hut and Father Paisios paused before entering. He turned to Kellan and met his gaze with an intense look. "God Who dwells in heaven is willing to dwell in a humbled heart. Can there be any greater humility than that shown by God Himself?" He smiled and gently patted Kellan once more on the head. "I have something I want to show you." He turned and led the way into the dark of the cell. He placed the potatoes next to the stove and rubbed the soil from his fingers. He lifted open the lid of the wooden box and reached inside, pulling something out that Kellan couldn't quite see in the shadows.

"These are the writings of my elder," he explained. "He gave them to me before he died."

Kellan looked closely but could only make out what looked like a bundle of old rags. He leaned closer and realised there were writings on the cloths but the loose bundle appeared shabby and barely worth any attention.

"I will give them to you before you leave Kellan, they will be of great assistance to you."

Kellan had no desire to be lumbered with this worthless item and began to protest.

"I couldn't take them Father, they mean too much to you."

"They are of no use to me, I cannot read."

Kellan was shocked to learn this; he had witnessed Father Paisios reciting the words of different services and even the Psalter without hesitation. "But what about the services? I have heard you."

"Father Ephraim made me learn everything by heart, the books you have been using were all his. I was a slow learner, but he showed great care and patience with me. I even resisted, but he knew what would be needed once he was gone."

Kellan took the rags being offered to him but didn't know what to say. He looked again at the lines scrawled across them and wondered if this was some kind of joke the old man was playing. But as Father Paisios turned and began preparing their food Kellan realised he was serious. He placed the bundle next to his bunk and joined Father Paisios at the stove. In silence they worked to make a meal from the few vegetables and Kellan tried to imagine how life must have been for the young Paisios here with his elder. It created a different sense of him and Kellan no longer just saw the old monk he had come to know. Here was the product of a whole lifetime, a man shaped by the bending his own will, who had trained himself through countless hours of prayer in order to find a peace Kellan had lived so many years without knowing even existed.

The large potatoes would take a couple of hours to bake in the little oven which was time Father Paisios always insisted he have to be alone. Kellan sat outside the hut, aware of how much weight he had lost and yet how much healthier he felt than when he lived in the village: it was though the old cravings of hunger had left him. His mind wandered back to the meals his sister would cook for him and the satisfaction she always got seeing his cleared plate. For the first time since he had come to the forest he began to weep. His chest shook with the sobs as he remembered her love for him and the way he had so casually taken her for granted, even seeing her as a burden at times. The tears that fell down his cheeks were not bitter or self-pitying, for the first time he wept without any concern for himself.

As the evening grew dark he looked at the hut and knew he would soon have to make a decision about leaving. Father Paisios' garden could never support them both through the winter and just as importantly, he knew in his heart that no matter how much he wanted the things Father Paisios spoke about, he himself was not a monk. He had stumbled on something important and he believed it was God who had brought him here, but he could feel no calling from God to stay.

Without warning the images of the attack on the village filled his mind's eye and instinctively he began to pray. The painful thoughts left him and he continued to repeat the phrases Father Paisios had taught him. Just as the old man had assured him, the strength of the episodes was weakening as he responded with prayer and with darkness now creeping into the forest he sat silently on the tree stump aware of God's love for him for which he felt a deep gratitude.

Chapter 6

Kellan woke to the sound of a woman's scream. His sweat-soaked body jolted under the blanket, a violent spasm tightening his muscles. The voice was familiar but he couldn't place it and with it came the memories of how the women of his village had suffered before their deaths. He sat up shaking, the cold of the night clinging to his damp skin.

Father Paisios appeared at his side, he held Kellan's arm and reassured him.

"It's alright; it was just a fox crying in the dark."

"I thought it was..." Kellan began to sob uncontrollably.

Father Paisios had a pan of water that was still hot and prepared some tea. Kellan took it gratefully, "I'm tormented even in my sleep Father."

"We are vulnerable at that time Kellan, relax, drink your tea and then join me in prayer when you feel ready."

Father Paisios returned to his usual place before the glowing oil lamp and began to pray loud enough that Kellan could follow the words. Once the tea was gone he quietly stood beside the old man but made no attempt to find the service in the book. He had no desire to say anything; it was enough to allow Father Paisios' words to speak for him. He made each line of prayer his own, and every so often a certain phrase would cut like a dagger to the very core of his feelings.

Hours passed this way until Father Paisios saw how tired the younger man was. He cut his own prayers short out of concern and motioned for Kellan to sit on the wooden box.

"I will make you some more tea," he said. "You must rest."

"How can I be so tired Father? Forgive me, but you are much older and yet you are always at prayer whenever I wake."

"Exhaustion can be caused by many things, not just physical labour; rest now, the water is nearly boiled."

"Why do you allow yourself so little sleep Father?"

"I deny myself bodily rest in order that I may discover spiritual rest. When the body is subdued and deprived of its pleasures the soul can find heavenly joys."

"But why must we deny ourselves something so natural and necessary?"

"There are those who become martyrs by laying down their lives for the love of Christ," explained Father Paisios. "But when no enemy's blade threatens our throat we can still offer our body in martyrdom by denying its desires: asceticism is a living martyrdom when it is accomplished for no other reason than love of God."

Steam curled as Father Paisios poured the water into the cups. The bitter tea brought Kellan to his senses a little and he felt his mind clearing. Father

Paisios remained standing as they drank and even now his lips moved as he silently prayed.

"What will become of me Father? Can I ever be healed of this?"

"Do not begin to allow self-pity to take hold of you," his voice was tender despite his reprimand. "Whatever happens we must not lose heart."

"Forgive me Father, but does God allow you to see what is yet to come?"

"Such things are for the saints Kellan, not for the likes of me. But we do not need the gift of foresight to see what awaits each of us."

"What do you mean Father?"

"Our souls will be called to account, with absolute certainty we must know this. Therefore let us live in preparation for the judgement which will determine our reward for all eternity."

"I do believe Father, but my grief overtakes me."

"We must remember that we suffer only for a short time in this world. When we grieve we must know that all earthly tears will pass away. Therefore let us not weep like children over the burdens of this life, but let our souls weep for the many sins we have committed. We must shed spiritual tears so that when we stand before God He will know that we are truly sorry for the evil we have done. Remember Kellan, the wailing on judgement day will be bitter and full of regret." Father Paisios paused for a moment and a serene expression filled his face, "To know these things we do not need any mystical gift of clairvoyance."

"I do believe Father; I know in my heart that all that you say is true."

"But knowing what is to come will not save us: only if we act on the knowledge will we be saved, we must repent while God gives us time."

He took the empty cup from Kellan's hand and began to swill it clean with water poured from a jug. "It is nearly time for you to continue your journey; you know you are not called to settle here. You need to have people around you; it is in your nature."

"Yes, but where will I go?"

"Do you have any relatives you can stay with?"

"No Father, my sister and I were the last of our family. I have no one."

"There is a place you could go, a town I visited many years ago. There is a priest who visits the forest once each year to bring me Holy Communion; he has told me about the road that leads there."

"Where is it Father?"

"I can give you directions, but you will only reach it if you follow my instructions." They walked out into the early morning air, a shock of cold cut through their clothing. "The year is moving on Kellan, if you are going to travel you will need to set off soon. It is no good setting out in sunshine only to be caught by the snow. But there are things we must discuss before you leave, you have begun to heal, but your wounds are still fresh."

Hearing Father Paisios speak about his departure made Kellan nervous. He knew he couldn't stay but the comfort of being with him would be something he would find hard to leave behind. And for reasons he couldn't explain he felt safe here, even from the bandits.

Father Paisios abruptly cut short their conversation and headed off to work in the garden. Kellan watched him disappear along the path into the trees and without considering any work he could be doing sat down on one of the stumps. He stared up at the patch of clear blue sky above him and began to think through all that had been said to him. As he reflected on his situation he understood the time was right to move on. Anxiety was prompting him to find an excuse to stay, but he knew Father Paisios was right. In the short time he had spent here he had learned to trust the old man's advice and knew that his own desires would only get in the way. He looked at the simple hut and smiled, realising how it would have looked to him just a few months before. But where he would once have seen a hovel, he now saw refuge.

Chapter 7

It was another two days before the topic of Kellan's departure was discussed again. He had begun to wonder if Father Paisios had changed his mind but then as they sat early in the morning drinking tea outside the hut the old man addressed the issue.

"There are some important things we must talk about before you leave. You are much stronger than when I found you but there are still many dangers that could threaten you."

"I feel as strong as an ox Father." And it was true; there was an energy within him that he had rarely known even in his life back in the world. Back then he had spent countless hours in the fields, but his sense of resentment and desire to be elsewhere always left him drained. Labour now was a new experience, an expression of something inner, an outward manifestation of his obedience and growing peace.

"I am not talking about your ability to lift weights," Father Paisios was a little curt, "there are many strengths and your muscles are the least of them."

Kellan knew this to be true, the small aging figure before him had revealed in these past weeks a strength he hadn't imagined existed. It was the power of human will that overcame every physical obstacle. Kellan fell silent, Father Paisios' tone made it clear that what he had to say was important.

"If you are to do battle you must wear the right armour, or else the enemy will easily strike you down." He leaned towards the younger man to convey his seriousness. "If you do the enemy's work for him he won't need to lift a finger to harm you because you'll already have wounded yourself."

Kellan resisted the urge to ask questions, he sensed the importance of the moment even if he wasn't sure he would grasp everything that was said to him.

"You must make a journey, but your heart must be shielded from what is to come or else you will never arrive at your destination."

Kellan could hold his tongue no longer, "What kind of shield do you mean Father?"

"It consists of two great metals blended for strength. The first is unpolluted humility, and the second is the willingness to forgive."

Kellan had learned enough from the old man to recognise a little of the value of these virtues, but he would never have guessed that these would be the great lesson he would be sent away with.

"These words are familiar to you Kellan, but you must go beyond what you think you know so that humility and forgiveness may genuinely grow within you. Unless you carry these two into battle you will not survive. Only a fool rides into battle defenceless, and he will be the first to fall."

Father Paisios looked down at the ground as he gathered his thoughts, this final teaching was too important to rush or risk confusing. "First Kellan you must learn to forgive even to the extent of not secretly hoping that God will punish the wrongdoer. If we pretend to forgive while harbouring the desire for divine punishment on our persecutors then it is no kind of forgiveness at all. And without forgiveness every blow and arrow of the enemy will find their target. It is vital that you understand this Kellan, where you are going will demand this of you."

ouch

"I accept this Father, but how should I work to achieve it beyond prayer?"

"True forgiveness is found when we genuinely let go of all anger and want only good for those who harm us. I see in your face you are not yet ready to forgive those who attacked your people, but we must strive to see the person beyond the evil that they perform, even as we ask God to see us beyond our sins. Any kind of condemnation is the fruit of our having judged others and if we fill our hearts with judgement we call God's judgement on ourselves. We can only do this by seeing that those who wrong us only make themselves into victims: evil action has an eternal effect on the one who performs it unless they repent, whereas our suffering that comes from the actions of others is transient."

"Forgive me Father, but you don't know the pain the bandits have caused me."

"Do not presume that your heart is the only one to be injured. I have lost someone I loved too, my Elder meant more to me than any earthly, natural father could be. When we were near the edge of the forest meeting a priest who brought us bread we were attacked by bandits. Elder Ephraim enabled me to escape but gave up his life to save me."

"I am so sorry Father, I didn't realise he died fighting these people."

"No, not fighting, a great miracle was given to us through his prayers. The bandits fell upon us without warning, they seemed to come from every direction, and immediately Elder Ephraim began to pray. He made no attempt to seek the safety of the forest but simply knelt and prayed. I remember the impression it made on me, in that moment of terror, seeing him so calm and immediately turning to God. Suddenly there appeared a line of warriors who came from behind us and marched towards the bandits. As they were turning to run Elder Ephraim pointed to the path leading back to our cell and commanded me to escape. I did just that, like you Kellan, I wanted to save my skin and I took his command as my excuse to do so."

"What happened Father, how did they manage to kill him?"

"The bandits fled but not far away, they waited until Elder Ephraim ceased praying. As he made his way back home they fell upon him and murdered him."

"Why didn't his warriors protect him?"

"He prayed for angels to protect me Kellan, but gave no thought for his own life. As soon as I was safely away he accepted his fate without concern for what would happen to him."

Kellan stared at Father Paisios as he finished his story, it seemed impossible to believe, but he knew the old man would not lie. He didn't know what to say and was grateful when Father Paisios broke the silence once more: "You see Kellan, never lose hope. No matter what happens on your journey, never lose hope in God."

Kellan nodded, but was now a little afraid at what lay ahead of him.

"Come with me to the stream," said Father Paisios, "we should stroll a little and let these things sink in to that dense head of yours." The playfulness of the insult brought a smile to Kellan's face and he happily followed the old man along the path. As they approached the stream they could see a deer with its neck bent to drink. As the two men approached Kellan anticipated that the creature would bolt and feared it might charge at them. He came to a stop and watched as Father Paisios continued forward until he was alongside the creature. It rubbed its head into his chest and he patted the side of its neck with the flat of his hand. "Go on," he shouted, "get!" He pushed at the deer's shoulders, forcing it to turn away from him before it casually walked off following the path of the stream. Kellan now approached watching the animal disappear into the trees, slightly unnerved by the event.

Father Paisios sat on a fallen tree trunk and told Kellan to take a drink. The water was cold and clear as he cupped it to his mouth with his hand. He wiped his palm on his trouser leg and took his seat next to the old man. The sound of the running water was like a living voice along the floor of the forest, speaking life into the blood and sap of men, into animals and trees alike.

"Do you understand what I have told you about forgiveness?"

"I think so Father."

"It is vital that you remember these things. When we judge others we stop loving them. If even for a moment we consider ourselves superior to anyone else then we have become blind to our sins. When our neighbour stumbles we should feel compassion for them as they endure the attacks of our common enemy. When someone falls we must pray for them in their battle and know that we have stumbled many times ourselves. We must condemn only ourselves and truly see the evil in our hearts. Never let the enemy seduce you into judging anyone, because to do so is to hold the devil's hand as he leads you down the path of pride and delusion. To walk with him this way will be a great fall for you."

"I think I understand Father."

"Yes, the words are simple," admitted the old man, "but the doing is not so easy. You will know, you will know." They both looked down at the stream for a while, its movement relaxed them and filled the silence with a sense of ease.

"The second ingredient in your shield must be spiritual poverty. There can be no victory if you lack this."

"What do you mean by spiritual poverty Father?"

"We must be humble, even like a child who lives in simplicity, considering himself nothing. God blesses the humble beyond measure just as the proud drive themselves far away from God's grace." Elder Paisios looked over at him and watched his face carefully, assessing how much Kellan was listening. "Pray Kellan; call upon Christ's name constantly wherever you go."

"Is that sufficient Father? Is there anything more I should pray about?"

"What more can you ask for? Well God's assistance yes, but to do what? You must fill your prayers with a desire for genuine humility. Never seek signs or elated states, for in these the devil easily traps us. But in every breath let there be a longing for humility. Consider yourself unworthy of any good thing, and when God sees you humbled He will bless you with treasures beyond your imagining. But don't let these gifts be your goal, only humility itself must be the desire and craving of your soul."

Kellan knew that in the presence of Father Paisios prayer seemed so achievable and made his own resolve firm. But once he had left he wondered whether he would maintain his longing for God. He tried to express his concerns, "Father, it is easy to feel God in this desert you have created, but I am weak and the world has many distractions."

"The outer desert that you see is only a dim reflection of the inner desert that the monk must find within himself. You are not a monk, but you must find this space within you."

Kellan shook his head, "I don't know if I can."

"You can, for it is not in our own strength that we do this. No man could bring into being the internal desert without God's grace. Always remember this Kellan; we do nothing without God's help."

"I will try Father."

"The heart must become a barren place to every passion, so inhospitable that no sinful desire can ever take root there. The burning heat of the desert is generated by constant prayer of the heart, the rocky ground is sleepless vigils and asceticism, self-denial, fasting and every spiritual endeavour that make the passions flee."

"But how can a desert be a good thing to cultivate within oneself, isn't it a lifeless place?"

"No," Father Paisios' voice was gentle. "See how the Egyptian wilderness was inhabited by men of faith. The holy saints are the rich fruit that grows where no other harvest may be found. So in the desert of the heart there are godly hermits too: love and forgiveness must live there. Remember Kellan, salvation grows where the passions wither."

Father Paisios then stood and moved to the edge of the stream. "Come here Kellan, I want to show you something." Kellan moved to his side and looked to where the old man now pointed. "That," said Father Paisios "is your route out of the forest."

Kellan could just make out a lightly trod path heading away from them on the other side of the stream. "When you get near the edge of the forest the path will be lost. But you will see more of the sky where the forest thins, look for the sun and keep heading east. And no matter what, keep to the road and do not stop heading east. You must always head east."

As Father Paisios gave his directions Kellan was struck by the reality of what was happening and could feel his nerve leaving him. "I feel uneasy about leaving you Father."

"You need to see a bigger sky again Kellan, and there is a place up ahead of you that will make any hardship worth suffering."

"Where should I head Father? I have seen little beyond my village."

"When you leave the forest you will see a road. Follow this for a couple of weeks; you will know when you have reached your destination."

"A couple of weeks," Kellan's exclamation betrayed his feelings. "What will I eat?"

"Your question is born of a lack of faith, how many times have I told you that God will provide."

"But I have heard stories of people starving on the roadside Father, forgive me, but I need to know what I am to do."

"Come back to my cell Kellan, I will equip you with all that you will need." With that he turned and at a brisk pace headed for home. Kellan trotted behind, still a little concerned at the prospect of such a long journey without provisions.

At the hut Father Paisios instructed Kellan to sit while he disappeared into his cell. A few moments later he emerged with a collection of items that he offered to Kellan.

"This is a piece of bread that has dried and will need soaking before you eat it. Break off a small piece each day. It is blessed by a priest and will keep you strong." He then produced the shabby bundle of Elder Ephraim's writings.

"These are richer in wisdom than anything I have been able to share with you," said Father Paisios. "I have been a dim reflection of what he taught me, but here you will read words for yourself from his holy mouth."

Kellan politely took them and laid them beside the bread in a rough cloth the old man had given him to tie them up in. The old man then handed him the leather water flask that Kellan had brought with him into the forest. The sight of it immediately reminded him of his life in the village before the attack.

"You will need a stick," Father Paisios announced and disappeared once more into the darkness of the hut. He returned with a simple length of stick that had been cut from a branch. It looked solid and Kellan liked the idea of having something he could defend himself with if necessary. Father Paisios raised the stick to eye level and seemed to be considering it carefully. "No," he muttered, and disappeared yet again into the hut. When he re-appeared he was carrying a beautifully carved stick of aged wood. The handle was ornately carved to resemble a dog's head and Kellan was surprised not to have seen it before.

"This was made by Elder Ephraim," Father Paisios explained. "It will get you to where you need to go."

"Thank you Father, I am grateful to you."

"Yes, it is a good stick, but my hiking days are behind me."

"No I mean for everything Father, including my life."

"Yes, yes," Father Paisios dismissed Kellan's words with a wave of his hand. "We must pray before you leave."

Kellan left everything he had been given on the tree stump and followed him into the cell. They made the sign of the cross together and Father Paisios began to pray.

"Holy Saviour, bless this boy on his journey, guard him from the enemy and give him wisdom to know your will. Holy Mother pray for us, Amen". The old man crossed himself once more, kissed the base of the painting and then left the cell. Although Kellan was now accustomed to praying he found he could add nothing more to the old man's simple prayer. He too made the sign of the cross over himself and gazed into the face of the Mother of God as she held her son. Kellan prayed within himself, "Hold me too Holy Mother."

Kellan found Father Paisios waiting for him outside. He handed him his new stick once more, and Kellan struggled to find the right words to express himself. But before he could say anything Father Paisios said "Remember what you have learned here, God be with you." And with that he turned and abruptly went back into his cell before Kellan could utter another word. For a moment Kellan stood staring at the door, wondering if the old man was about to emerge once more. But the door remained shut and he understood that the monk had said all that he was going to say, his farewell had been completely without sentimentality, there was nothing more he needed to add. It saddened Kellan to leave this way but accepting Father Paisios' wishes he turned and headed toward the stream. The path was now very familiar to him and he wondered if he would ever walk this way again. At the stream he carefully stooped and filled the flask before stepping from one bank to the other to find the path to which Father Paisios had pointed. He was grateful for the stick as he made his way through the undergrowth but unlike his first day in the forest he now had no fear of this place. The sense of walking alone made him aware of the differences in him since that day he had come here but also that he still carried the shame and grief that hadn't died within him but at least now was something he felt he understood.

He had been on the move for a couple of hours when he realised that he could no longer be sure if he was following the path. He looked up and saw more of the blue sky than he had seen for a long time. He calculated his direction from the position of the sun and continued to head east. The space between the trees was widening and his pace quickened. After another half hour or so he could see open space up ahead of him through the trees and he began to trot. He felt excited to be returning to the world outside the forest and for a moment at least he felt no fear of what awaited him.

At last he broke through the tree line and found himself looking up a steep pasture at the top of which was a line of hedges that suggested a road. Out in the open the sky seemed huge and he gazed up at the few clouds that lazily drifted overhead. He tied the bundle of cloth to the end of the stick and lifted it over his shoulder. At the top of the hill he looked back at the forest and was amazed at its vastness. It stretched off beyond the horizon and he thought of the little hut hidden in its depths and the monk he was sure would now be praying for him.

The road was dry and firm and satisfying himself that there was nothing moving in either direction he turned his back to the west and began to walk.

Chapter 8

The early morning cold had been replaced with midday warmth as Kellan strode along the road heading east. He had been walking without a break and yet felt no sense of tiredness. Every so often thoughts and images would wriggle their way into his mind but each time he calmly recognised their presence and returned to praying. The steady rhythm of his legs counted time for the inner words to God and the combination of physical activity and prayer created a sense in him of his whole being focussed in a single activity of drawing closer to the One he knew was with him.

As the road climbed to the crest of a small hill Kellan took the opportunity to look back at the view and assess how far he had travelled. There was no sight of the forest and to the horizon there stretched a scene of rolling hills and fields. Other than the road there was no sign of human activity which gave Kellan the feeling of being the last man alive on earth. He turned and looked at the road before him, estimating how steep the path would become and imagining himself walking through the fields he could see ahead. With Father Paisios now far away Kellan's concern for bandits began to return and he scanned the world around him in every direction looking for anything that might suggest danger. But there was nothing that concerned him and satisfied that he was safe he sat and drank some water. He wondered how far the journey would take him and with these thoughts came a little anxiety which he quickly dismissed before returning to prayer. He hung the flask back over his shoulder and set off once more.

By the time early evening was approaching Kellan was beginning to feel tired. Beneath the shade of a large tree in a field next to the road he dropped to the ground and rested his back against its trunk. As he looked around at the field before him he noticed that the branches of some of the trees were laden with apples. Excitedly he trotted over to them and reached up to pull some of the fruit free. With half a dozen pushed into his sack he selected a final apple and walked back to his place in the shade. Thanking God for the gift he inspected the fruit with great care, almost feeling a sense of awe at its beauty. But its appearance was nothing compared to the taste as he bit into it. Juices filled his mouth and the natural sugars reminded him of how long it had been since he last enjoyed anything sweet. He ate it down to the core and quickly followed it with another. He caught himself smiling with a deep sense of satisfaction, and realised how foolish he would appear to anyone who could see him now. Sitting in the middle of nowhere with just wild apples for dinner and nowhere to take shelter for the night, what could he possibly have to grin about? To the world he was a poor lost fool, but in his heart he knew there was nothing more he needed. Outwardly he had all he could want; only painful memories had the capacity to destroy what he felt.

He was then startled by a throaty call from somewhere up above him in the branches of the tree. He twisted to find its source and spotted a black crow looking down at him. The bird called out again and Kellan knew it was a cry directed at his presence. The crow sat motionless and Kellan called up to him "You've got to share your apples now."

He remembered the bundle of rags on which Elder Ephraim had recorded his teachings and decided to read a little. Kellan laid the sack out on the ground and untied it so that it once more became a large cloth square. As he did so he saw that what he had expected to be a miserable collection of rags now looked more ordered and cleaner than he had thought and the words were clearly legible. He put the change in appearance down to the dark of the forest as opposed to the bright sunlight which now illuminated everything around him. He began at the first page, and in a simple but elegant handwriting it read: *When a man's heart is darkened with passions he will only see darkness around him: for example a suspicious heart will see suspicion even in that which is pure.*

Kellan laid the writings back on to the cloth and allowed the meaning to shape his thoughts. He told himself to resist the anxieties his fears might suggest and relaxed to enjoy the rest his body was now taking. He closed his eyes and in a few minutes had fallen to sleep.

He woke some hours later in pitch darkness. The sky was cloudless and filled with an unimaginable number of stars. The temperature had dropped and Kellan buttoned his coat with annoyance at himself for having slept so long. He gazed up at the stars and found the familiar constellations he had known since he was a boy. The patterns always spoke to him of timelessness; he knew they would be the same when he was an old man looking up at them, and even when he was dead and long gone others would see the very same stars in the exact same patterns. There had been times when he had been walking home drunk and the sight of the stars had sobered him into seeing his place in the universe. And now he understood that while walking through the daylight the stars had always been there, he had simply been unable to see them. The sky was always full of stars, but the intense light of the sun made them invisible.

As he contemplated the sky the screech of an owl pulled him back to the field in which he sat and he got to his feet feeling an ache in his back. He stretched out the tension from his muscles and gathered his things together. Satisfied that he had had enough sleep he decided to walk in the dark since the moon's silver light gave a crisp clarity to the ground and he felt confident of his footing. He found two more apples in the tree which he stuffed into his pockets and then made his way back to the road. The stars were a familiar guide to him and reassured him that the road was taking him east.

Through the dark he walked now alert to the sounds of the night. With the horizons gone his sense of the world was in the call of foxes and the panicked rustle of animals as they became startled at his approach. His footsteps sounded much louder and he was aware of his breathing as he filled his lungs with the cold night air. The walking soon warmed him and he was able to focus his mind to prayer without distraction. He knew that the small lamp would be glowing in Father Paisios' cell and he felt united to him as they prayed despite the miles between them.

All was well until Kellan heard movement on the road behind him. He froze in fear and strained to see into the black night. His whole body became alert to any sign of someone approaching but there was no repeat of the sound. He stood there for a while longer, wondering if someone was just out of view watching him and preparing to rush him. But no attack came and he began to relax, convincing himself he had only heard an animal out on its hunt. He waited a few more minutes before continuing on but now he made an effort to tread lightly, his attention now entirely focussed on everything that his ears told him about the world.

Eventually Kellan knew he needed more sleep and realising that there were still some hours before sunrise he began to look for somewhere to lie down. He spotted a field of long grass sloping down from the road and headed off into it, taking large strides in order to avoid leaving a clear trail to where he was. Once he was happy that he was far enough away from the road he bedded down in the soft grass with his bundle beneath his head. The smell of the grass reminded him of harvest and its familiarity added to his growing feeling of security. He curled himself against the cold but also to become as small as possible as though it would make him impossible to find and despite his anxieties he had no trouble falling quickly to sleep.

Chapter 9

The sunrise caught Kellan an hour's walk from where he had woken. The orange sky was a welcome sign of daylight and a promise of the warmth it would bring. As he covered the miles Kellan was preoccupied with something his sister had once said about him and though he knew it was silly to be concerned over something so trivial he couldn't let go. The sound of her voice was as real to him as anything he could hear around him. The memories began to lead him through a list of people and events and there was even an element of joy as he recalled them, but inevitably they led him to one inescapable moment in time and his mood became as black as the charred houses he visualised.

It was in this state that he pushed himself to climb a steep rise in the road that was draining his energy. As he made the summit of the hill he paused to catch his breath. Looking down over the fields before him his stomach tightened in horror as he tried to take in what he was seeing. About half a mile further down the road was the remains of a village. Every building had been burned and smashed and the dark remains immediately conjured before him once more the violence of the attack on his own village. He stood rooted to the spot, staring at the disfigured remains, looking without hope for signs of life. Everything was still and he could see there was no way to follow the road without passing through the site. He calculated how far he would have to skirt around to avoid the village but in the end decided to risk going straight through.

The road gently descended towards the village and as he got closer Kellan realised that the attack had happened a long time before. The buildings were not just burned but some of them had begun to collapse in the wind and rain: he felt safer knowing that whoever had done this was no doubt far away by now.

At the edge of the village he was overcome with a terrible sadness at the sight of this place where people had lived out their lives now broken and abandoned. Unlike his own village so soon after the attack there was now nothing left lying around that might be useful to him, scavengers had obviously stripped the place of everything they could carry. He tried to estimate how many people might have been here and suspected it could have been as high as fifty or sixty. He overcame his impulse to run and walked calmly through the village, feeling he shouldn't look too long into the open sides of homes where private spaces were now exposed and violated.

He was nearly through when he noticed a figure sitting at the far edge of the village on the remains of a fence. It was a man, bent forward staring at the ground. Kellan wondered how the stranger couldn't have seen him coming and looked around to see if he was alone. There was no sign of others but taking no chances, before approaching him Kellan shouted "Hey!"

The man slowly raised his head and looked without response back at him. Kellan was unsure what to do and without thinking about it waved his hand to him. This time the figure responded with a raised hand and hesitantly Kellan headed towards him. The man stared blankly at Kellan's approach, not giving signs of fear or suspicion.

As he drew closer Kellan could see the man was hideously undernourished, his clothes were little more than rags and his unkempt hair and beard gave the impression of a man who had been abandoned on a desert island.

"Hello!" Kellan called out before getting alongside him.

The man tilted his head back in a gesture of acknowledgement but said nothing.

Kellan judged the man to be of little threat and walked up to him, "Are you from this village?"

The man's face was crumpled and dirty; his pale, watery eyes looked drained of every grain of hope or joy. He gave a single nod and turned to continue staring at the ruins.

"Was it bandits?" Kellan persisted.

The man nodded once more but didn't look back at him.

"My village was attacked not long ago," Kellan added.

The man looked down at his bare feet. "They took my wife and children."

Kellan swallowed, he understood the man's grief. "They did the same to us. I found everyone dead."

The man turned to look at him, "They left the bodies behind?"

"No, I mean they killed everyone and I found the village empty."

"How do you know they are dead? How can you be sure?"

Kellan couldn't bring himself to admit he had watched some of the attack, "I saw the marks where they had dragged the bodies. There was blood."

"I can't be sure my wife is dead, but I don't know how to find her."

Kellan knew that it was better for her to now be dead than still alive in the hands of these men but couldn't tell him so. "How long ago was the attack?"

"Many months, I'm not sure how long."

"Months!" Kellan repeated back at him, "You have been here all this time?"

"I was away, I was a trader, I came back and found...this. I have been here ever since."

"How have you stayed alive?"

"There is an orchard they didn't find over the hill, I have been living off its fruit." The man's voice was monotone and dry.

"What will you do?" Kellan asked.

"Do? What do you mean?" The man looked genuinely confused by the question.

"Where will you go?"

The man stared out at the village, "I will stay here in case my wife or children return."

"I don't think they will come back."

The man spun his head, "How can you know that? Who are you to say this?"

"From what I have seen, I'm sorry, but I don't think they will return."

The man grew angry, "Shut up, you don't know what you're talking about. If they're alive they will make their way back home. Where else do you think they would go?"

"I...I don't know, I'm sorry." Kellan couldn't tell him what he knew to be true.

"You're sorry?" There was still anger in the man's voice. "What right do you have to be sorry? Who are you to feel anything? You didn't know them; keep your sorry to yourself."

Kellan looked at him, there didn't seem anything he could say or do to help. He sat down on the fence beside him and offered him his flask. The man looked at it for a moment and then took it and drank some of the water. It seemed to calm him and his voice became a little more measured. "Thank you," he half whispered.

They sat in silence for a short while then the man asked "Why are you here?"

"I'm passing through; this is just the way I'm going."

"Where exactly?

Kellan shook his head, "I'm not sure, there's a place I'm heading to."

"What's it called?"

"I don't know," Kellan admitted, "but it's somewhere on this road."

"I've travelled up and down this road for years," the man said. "Which town are you wanting to reach?" He seemed irritated by Kellan's lack of an answer.

"Like I said, I don't know."

The man was growing suspicious, "Tell me who you are."

"My name is Kellan, my village was attacked, and now I'm heading east."

The man handed back the water flask and got to his feet. He walked away from Kellan and stood with his back to him. Kellan thought he was about to say something but again he fell silent.

"Are you going to be alright?" Kellan asked, but there was no response. He stood motionless, staring at the destroyed buildings.

Kellan took a drink of water and watched the back of the man's head, wondering what he could say or do to help him.

Suddenly the man shouted "Look what they did! Look at it!" There was now no anger in his voice, only a bemused confusion, a tone that pleaded for explanation."

"I know," said Kellan, "they did the same to us."

"Look what the bastards did," the man shouted, but even now his voice was filled with confusion.

Kellan recognised his own pain in the man before him, but knew he couldn't allow himself to respond in this way to their loss. "If you stay here you'll die. They're not coming back." He spoke in a matter-of-fact tone that somehow reached the man

"I know," he said, "I don't care."

He turned and Kellan saw the truth of this in his face. A huge part of him was dead already and he had no desire to find a way of carrying his burden. Their eyes met and Kellan had to look away, the emptiness in the man's eyes drained him of hope and nothing in this world could meet his need. Kellan silently prayed for him and then stood to leave.

"I am sorry this has happened, I understand what it means." Kellan reached out to touch the man's arm but he recoiled and stepped back from him.

"They're gone," the man repeated, "everyone."

"Not everyone," said Kellan, "you're still alive."

The man frowned back at him; they both knew this was only half true.

Kellan swung the water flask back over his shoulder and picked up his stick and sack. He turned to the man once more but he had already resumed his staring out across the remains of the village.

"Are you sure you're going to stay?" Kellan asked. But there was no response.

"Goodbye," said Kellan as he turned and headed back to the road. On the other side of the village Kellan looked back to see the man still motionless, sitting on the fence where he had left him. Despite his concern for the man it was a relief to be leaving and Kellan wondered how long he would survive here once the winter months arrived.

Kellan walked for another two hours before stopping for water. The meeting had troubled him and he knew he needed to calm himself. He pulled out Elder Ephraim's writings and turned to the next page. He was startled to find the words spoke to his very concerns:

Draw close to those who suffer and you will find God because he is always near to those in pain. When we begin to think only of the pain of our neighbour and see our own struggles as nothing we discover it is not a stranger we carry but Christ Himself.

Kellan didn't know what he could have done for the man in the village. He had chosen to die there, he had given up. Kellan saw that there was nothing the man would allow him to do for him, and then he recognised the one thing possible: he prayed for him.

Chapter 10

The encounter continued to make Kellan feel uneasy. Grief was no longer something that afflicted just him and this realisation made it more difficult to cope with. He didn't understand why this was, but he knew the pain was not something he could overcome alone, even if he found peace within himself there would still be others who suffered. The death of his fellow villagers had brought their experience to an end; they were no longer victims to the barbarity of the world. He realised that this had made it at least a little easier to bear, but now he saw that there were others who lived on like himself. Accepting that this was no longer his suffering alone forced him to recognise that he was merely one small part of what was happening. He felt a little diminished by this, as though it had helped to think of his pain as somehow unique or special. But the truth was he was one victim among many and the universe had no obligation to treat him with any particular concern.

He kept walking even when he was exhausted in order to put as much distance between himself and the burned village. Even as the evening was growing dark he forced himself on. As the road passed between high hedges he found the deep shadows hid enough obstacles to keep tripping him up and he knew he had to rest for the night. He used his stick to prod the ground before him and carefully continued to where the surrounding fields opened up once more. He cut back a little behind the hedgerow to make sure he was completely out of sight from the track and sat down on the dry earth. There was little vegetation here but a shallow ditch provided a comfortable place to bed down and he felt safe being hidden even further from view.

He ate the last of the apples and washed it down with gulps of water. He then broke off a small piece of died bread that Father Paisios had placed in amongst his things. Soaked in a little water it felt like a feast. It was comforting to be filling his belly and he stretched out to relax. He tried to estimate the distance he had travelled by calculating how many hours he had been moving. He felt a certain satisfaction when he realised he must have covered nearly thirty miles that day. He wondered how far he still had to go and began to think about where he would find more food. There were plenty of streams to fill his flask from, but hunger would become a problem if he didn't eat while walking. He then remembered the words of Father Paisios, "God will provide." He trusted in this promise and regained his sense of peace.

At that moment the familiar cry of a crow came out of the darkness. It couldn't possibly be the same one he had heard before, no crow would follow someone like that and he hadn't seen it as he walked. But the sound was exactly as it had been before and it unnerved Kellan a little. He reached out and griped his stick, positioning it so that he could swing it from where he was lying. But nothing happened to call on such manoeuvres and the day's exercise was rewarded with an easy sleep.

The following morning Kellan discovered he was in a small meadow that was surrounded by different kinds of trees. Many of their leaves had turned golden brown and the ground was covered in dew. The early morning sunshine sparkled through countless spiders' webs that hung between the tufts of tall grass. The scene was other-worldly and took Kellan out of himself as he marvelled at its beauty. It prompted him to open Elder Ephraim's writings and in the magic of the moment the pages had taken on a smooth appearance without any sign of crease or smudge. Kellan turned to the page he had marked with a thread of cotton from his jacket and began to read.

The devil dresses his traps as the sweetest of pleasures, his troops as the warmest of friends. Do not be deceived by either: remain watchful over everything that you permit into your heart. There are many doors into the heart and mind and the spiritual struggler must keep guard over all of them. The eyes will rest on many delights that inflame the heart with desire; the ears are bombarded with flattery and heresy: all of these will lead the unwary into what appears to be a beautiful garden but reveals itself to be the first chambers of hell.

Kellan smiled at the thought of anything bringing pleasure out here on the road but understood that his soul was being filled with unwanted thoughts and images. He made a decision to use the day as an opportunity for focussing his mind on what would be allowed in within him and carefully folded the writings back into his sack.

The ditch had kept him protected from the wind and he was fully refreshed from the night's sleep. He gathered his things and looked around for the crow he had heard. It wasn't to be seen but the songs of other birds drifted across the meadow. He found his way back to the road and once more set off.

At around midday he heard the sound of running water and decided to fill his flask. He followed the sound to a small brook that looked as clear as water from a well. He scooped an initial handful to test it and was pleased with the result. It was cold and fresh and he emptied the little water that remained in his flask in order to fill it afresh. He screwed the top tight and laid it beside his jacket and other belongings on a large rock beside the stream. Taking off his boots he waded into the water which was no deeper than a little above his ankles and began to search for fish. He stood still, hoping not to reveal his presence to any that might be near and surveyed the bed of the stream by bending low over it, ready to snatch his dinner. He knew it took patience and was ready to spend as much time as it demanded now that he had set his mind on eating a decent meal.

But his plan was cut short by the sound of approaching voices. They were already close as they approached from the direction of the road. Kellan instinctively dived towards the opposite bank and threw himself into the cover of the bushes there. As he lay listening he realised he had left his things in clear view but it was now too late to retrieve them. He tried to decide whether this would prompt those approaching to search for him and whether he should make a run for it. But the voices were now close and he remained flat on his stomach, unable to see through the leaves to the other bank.

A man was giving instructions about filling water bags but Kellan couldn't make out how many there were. If they were bandits they would likely want to find him when they saw his belongings, but either way he knew he was unlikely to get his things back whoever they were. He cursed himself for leaving them out of reach, but concern for his own safety was even more pressing.

He listened to them splashing about in the water and laughing. There was a woman amongst them and their playfulness surprised him. He took it as a good sign, they weren't hunting him and it didn't sound like they were in the mood for violence. Then his own mood changed again when he heard one of the men shout "Look at that."

He heard them moving towards where he had left his things and now it could only be a matter of time before they began searching for him. His hiding place wouldn't conceal him for more than a few minutes if they were serious about finding him and he began to think through how he should react. He had no weapon, and against however many there were he stood little chance of overcoming them. He resigned himself to the inevitable and began to pray.

But his expectations were proved groundless when he heard one of the men calling out.

"If you're hiding come out, we won't harm you."

Kellan stayed where he was, trying to decide why bandits would bother with such a tactic.

Another man then shouted "Show yourself, we won't hurt you."

Kellan slid from under the bushes and got to his feet. He stepped out into view and saw three men and a woman looking back at him. None of them were armed with anything more than a staff; they had the appearance or ordinary villagers, perhaps farmers, but certainly not bandits. Kellan felt relief flood through him, he stepped closer, almost into the stream.

"Who are you?" The woman asked.

"I'm Kellan, I was just getting some water. I heard your voices and hid."

"Come over Kellan, we're not a threat." The man who was clearly some kind of leader of the group stepped forward and extended his hand. Kellan splashed through the water and reached out in return. They shook hands and the man announced he was called Oren and then introduced the other members of the group. They each nodded at their names and smiled broadly. "Where have you come from Kellan? Why are you here?" Oren asked.

Kellan briefly explained about his village and that he was heading to a town in the east. At the mention of the bandits the group exchanged glances which were impossible to decipher but there was nothing suspicious about them

"You must come back with us Kellan; our village is not far from here. We'll cook you something decent. I expect you're ready for a good meal after so much time on the road." The woman's invitation was not something he could turn down despite his desire to keep moving.

"Thank you," said Kellan, "that would be most welcome."

They handed him his belongings and once his boots were secure they led him towards their village. As they walked they asked about his trade and the villages he had seen along the road. Again when he described the destroyed village he had found they asked nothing more about it as though it were a subject of no interest to them. But despite this their company was friendly and it felt good being amongst people again. For the first time in so long Kellan felt the old sense of himself returning and he recognised traits in his conversation and manner that hadn't been seen since all had been well at home.

After less than an hour's walking the roofs of buildings could be seen above trees that surrounded the village. The tiles were bright orange and the houses were in a style Kellan hadn't seen before. As they entered the village all looked clean and well ordered but Kellan noted that there were no high fences or lookouts posted for security. It was as though the bandits didn't exist here and he wondered if they hadn't begun their attacks this far east. He wanted to question them about these things but their chatter was filled with more frivolous matters and he didn't feel able to interrupt them.

A few people came out to see the new arrival and Kellan was happy to recognise the common features of village life that exist everywhere. The typical mixture of ages and dress, the signs of farming and small scale manufacturing that let him know that this was not a community living in fear.

Oren introduced Kellan to a few people and gave a brief summary of the details Kellan had first shared with them. The warmth of welcome continued and Kellan was offered the opportunity to bathe before he ate. He gladly accepted and followed Oren into his house. A short, mouse-haired woman was introduced as Oren's wife and she proceeded to heat the water for Kellan's bath. Twenty minutes later he was lowering himself into the hot suds and he could feel the stress and aches being drawn from his body. Sleeping rough had taken its toll on him and he remembered what it was like to be a civilised man once again.

For a while after his bath Kellan was left to his own devices and sat and read from Elder Ephraim. Oren returned once more and seemed pleased to see Kellan looking refreshed. It was getting dark and good smells were drifting from the kitchen. Oren laid the table and invited Kellan to take a seat. They talked a little about Oren's work until large steaming pots appeared before them. Oren's wife proved to be an excellent cook and she had made every effort to produce something special for their guest. Kellan ate more food in a single sitting than he had for longer than he could remember. The food was rich and satisfying and left Kellan feeling sleepy. Oren insisted that he drink some wine and by the end of the meal Kellan was feeling a little woozy.

They remained at the table chatting about village life and Kellan began to wonder if this was the place Father Paisios had intended him to reach. He no longer made any attempt to refuse the wine offered him and the two men began to relax in one another's company, making jokes about the state he had been in when they found him.

Suddenly there was a loud thud on the roof and Oren's wife rushed in. She looked concerned but not panicked.

"What's that?" Kellan asked.

"Don't worry yourself," said Oren, "I have to see to something."

Oren went out quickly and Kellan could hear him climbing onto the roof. The sound of Oren loudly beating the roof with something filled the room. "What's he doing?" Kellan asked.

"It's alright, this happens some times, you mustn't worry." Oren's wife's words of assurance were accompanied with a look of uncertainty.

"But what's he doing? What's going on?" Kellan insisted. He moved towards the door but the small woman held his arm.

"No," she cried, "it's best if you stay indoors. Don't go out, you're safe here."

"Safe from what? What's happening?" Kellan pulled free from her grip and stepped outside. On the roofs of a number of houses men were beating out flames as arrows fell from the sky igniting fresh fires. The arrows came in pairs, leaving glowing trails behind them as they arced through the night sky. The men on the roofs were serious but Kellan was surprised at how calm they were.

"Do you have weapons?" Kellan shouted up to Oren.

Oren's fire was out and he stood erect looking around at the rest of the village. Again Kellan couldn't believe how calm he looked, and repeated his question. "Oren, where are your weapons stored?"

Oren eventually looked down at him, "Don't worry yourself, go inside, we'll soon have these fires out."

"But what about the bandits? We need to prepare for the attack." Kellan was beginning to panic; he had seen what they would do to these people. His frustration only mounted further when Oren laughed, "Go inside Kellan, really, have some more wine."

Kellan had no impulse to flee, but he knew he had to warn the other villagers. He ran along the street shouting "Arm yourselves, prepare for the attack!"

A few faces appeared at windows but the flow of people out into the street that he expected never materialised. Kellan couldn't understand what was happening, their reaction made no sense at all. He headed back to where Oren was now standing outside his house, "Why aren't your people preparing themselves? What's wrong with them? Don't they know what the bandits will do?"

Oren tried to calm him, "Don't panic Kellan, it's alright. They never attack."

"What do you mean? They've done this before?" Kellan was bemused.

"Oh yes, often, come inside. Really Kellan, you have nothing to fear, we are safe, come inside and drink some wine. I will explain everything to you." He headed into the house and Kellan was left standing alone in the street. He looked around and realised that the arrows had stopped falling. With the fires extinguished all seemed to have returned to normal. He listened for sounds of an approaching attack but all was quiet. Slowly he began to walk back to the house but before going in he scanned the scene one more time. There was no movement of any kind, the incident was over.

Back inside Oren was sitting at the table refilling their glasses. "Come on in Kellan; sit down, I told you, everything's alright."

"How can you know that they won't attack?"

"They never do, it's nothing to get worried about."

"How long have they been doing this?" Kellan asked.

"For a few years now, it happens every few weeks, or sometimes we go months without a visit. We are quite used to it."

"Every few weeks? How can you live with this? They will attack; it won't end with a few arrows. Your whole village is in danger."

Oren chuckled, "Yes, there were many people who thought that way when it all began. Some even left the village. But as time has gone on we've grown accustomed to it. They rarely cause any real damage, and so long as we don't cause them trouble we don't think things will escalate."

"This is madness, how can you live like this?" Kellan looked to Oren's wife for a reaction but she turned and went into the kitchen.

"It's not what any of us want, of course. We've tried leaving offerings to them. We leave cows and sheep outside the village on the hill where they fire from. They always take what is offered and we consider this a small price to pay for keeping our village safe."

"No Oren, they won't be satisfied with livestock I've seen what they do. They will kill everyone, your women will be raped before they die, you must listen to me, you must be ready to fight."

"Enough of this Kellan, I don't want to hear another word about what you think."

"Who can I speak to in the village? Do you have a village council?"

"We do, I am its head. We decided together that this is the best course of action. We have no room here for hot heads, we can't risk provoking them.

We will do anything to maintain our peace, even if it means paying a small price to these men."

Kellan stared in disbelief. "Oren, please listen to me, if you don't do something everyone in this village will be killed. If not for your own sake then think of your wife. You must take up arms or leave this place. Listen to me Oren, you must do something."

"I have given you hospitality Kellan. I have gladly shared my table with you. Please respect my wishes on this matter. We can live with their arrows. Our village has continued when others are no more. You must be able to see that it is working. So long as we make a small sacrifice to them they leave us in peace. Even now some of our men are taking an offering up the hill. We don't consider it any great price."

Kellan shook his head, "I can't stay here, I'm sorry."

"Don't be ridiculous; get a good night's sleep. Do you think your attack will happen tonight after all these years?"

"I don't know, but I've seen what they do. I have to go. Let me speak to the other villagers, I will take anyone who wishes to come with me. But we must get out of here."

"No" Oren was no longer willing to listen. "If you wish to leave then there's the door. But we can't have you causing unrest amongst our people. I worked so hard to calm people; you don't now what it was like at the beginning. The people listened to me; I will be remembered for what I did for them." Oren caught himself becoming proud; he added "We have created order here when others have fallen into chaos. We have found a way Kellan; I can't allow you to spread fear. We will give you provisions, we are good people, we wish you no harm. But our peace cannot be disrupted."

"I'll go then, but when the day comes you'll wish you had listened to me. I take no satisfaction in knowing I'm right, your fate doesn't have to be the one you're choosing. This peace you speak of is an illusion; I'm sorry Oren I can't stay."

Oren was true to his word and ensured that Kellan was provided with a good stock of food to take with him. He and his wife accompanied Kellan to near the edge of the village, as much to ensure he caused no trouble as much as a show of politeness. Before he left Kellan looked at the two of them, it was unbearable to see such foolishness. "Thank you for the provisions, God bless you." As he said this he saw a glimmer of fear in her face, the briefest flash of what was being hidden within her.

"He already has," Oren smiled, "and our peace is the greatest blessing of all." The two of them held one another as Kellan walked away, watching until he disappeared from view in the dark.

Chapter 11

It was a relief to be out of the village but knowing the bandits were close filled Kellan with dread. He convinced himself that he was safer alone in the dark rather than a sitting target back with the others, but once the light of the village faded he quickly began to feel vulnerable. He followed the road in the moonlight but realised that as it twisted round it was heading towards the hill from which the arrows had been fired. He stopped in the road and watched the outline of the hill against the sky, looking for any kind of movement. There was no sign of life and he tried to tell himself that if they had their livestock they'd probably have moved on by now. But he couldn't bring himself to go any further, and he didn't know what to do. He could hide in the hedges until morning but he knew he was too close to really be safe, and if they were still around they might be watching him even now. Besides, he wanted to get away from this place, the sense of impending danger was overwhelming, and he needed to remove himself from what he had no doubts was going to happen.

He crouched in the dark, all the time looking for movement around him. He remembered Father Paisios' instruction not to leave the road, but the idea of skirting around the hill and picking up the road on the other side was making more sense to him as he thought it through. He could use the stars to ensure he didn't get lost, and maybe in a few hours he'd be back on track. He had decided that staying here was definitely not an option, and he knew he didn't have the courage to keep going ahead. But then he rejected the thought of staying on the road, it wasn't a matter of courage; it made good sense not to deliberately walk up to the bandits and reveal himself. This wasn't a matter of cowardice he told himself, but logic and clear thinking.

He pushed his way through a low hedge and was off the road. The ground was uneven and slowed his progress but better to be slow than dead he thought. The shadows now looked more threatening than ever before, his imagination conjured up bandits all around and he felt the confidence leaving him like a physical presence departing his body. As the terrain became more difficult he could see that it would take most of the night to make it all the way round the hill and he allowed himself frequent breaks so that his breathing wouldn't become too laboured and loud.

The combination of cloud cover and thick undergrowth meant he had little sense of where he was in relation to the road and he began to curse himself when he acknowledged that he was lost. The stars were now completely hidden and the lack of moonlight plunged the world around him into even deeper darkness. He could hear Father Paisios' voice warning him not to leave the road and he tried to convince himself that he'd had no choice.

As he emerged into a flat meadow he began to pray. Not for humility or wisdom, but that God would protect him. He could offer nothing to God but the same impulses of the dumb creatures scurrying through the night. He felt ashamed to have become so base in his needs but still he implored God to watch over him.

From the bushes on both sides of him he suddenly saw the shape of men silently running towards him. It was impossible to judge how many but he could see immediately that there was no possibility of standing up to them. He spun round in panic trying to decide which direction to run but behind him he saw faces looming forwards and he knew it was too late.

At once hands grabbed at him from every direction and with them blows rained down on his head and shoulders. A punch to the side of the face knocked him sideways and he stumbled to the ground. The attackers began to kick him and he instinctively curled to protect himself. He heard himself let out an involuntary cry of pain and his body became limp and defenceless. The blows continued and he knew they intended to kill him.

But the violence stopped as a bright light approached, Kellan was still conscious enough to see a man approaching carrying a burning torch. The others moved back to let him near and as he reached Kellan he lifted his foot and dropped it heavily on his throat. Kellan gasped for air but the pressure only increased as he did so.

In the light of the torch he watched them unwrapping his sack. They snatched at the food and began biting like wild dogs. One of the bandits handed the man with the torch the bundle of Elder Ephraim's writings but he contemptuously threw it back to the ground. Another man then handed him the carved stick which he snapped over his knee and casually threw away.

Finally the man leaned close to Kellan's face, his foot still firmly pressing down on his throat. His breath was hot and bitter and he leered at Kellan with a vile expression that was filled with lust and greed. Kellan gripped the man's ankle but he was too weak to break free, and seconds later, to the sound of laughter, he passed out.

Chapter 12

It was a surprise to wake and still be alive. His throat felt crushed and every breath brought pain, not just in his neck but throughout his chest. As he tried to raise himself he realised his ribs were cracked and sharp pain pinned him back to the ground. He lay still, trying to focus his eyes on his surroundings but it was dark and he couldn't understand where he was. The ground beneath him was vibrating and he realised he was inside something that was moving.

He managed to roll slightly, clutching his side in a vain attempt to relieve the pain. He was inside some kind of wooden box; he could make out the dimensions by the odd streak of light that leaked through cracks in the side. It was not quite high enough for a man to stand upright in but looked large enough to hold about twenty people: though right now he was alone. Across the far end was a collection of items thrown into a pile. He couldn't make out the details but slid over to feel for anything that might be useful. He found his partially unfolded sack but it was empty and so he began feeling for his water flask. Every movement was accompanied by pain in his ribs but his thirst was unbearable. The water flask wasn't there but he did find Elder Ephraim's writings cast casually amongst the other items by someone who could only see worthless rags. He carefully folded the pages back into shape and laid them beside him, relieved to have kept what had been entrusted to him.

Without a window there was no way of knowing what time of day it was and this combined with the effects of the blows to his head left him disorientated. If his ribs would have allowed him he would have peered through one of the cracks to determine the source of light but it was impossible. He rolled the cloth sack into a pillow and lay on his back, trying to detect any sounds that might be a clue as to what was happening. He could hear some shouting and occasionally the same laughter he had heard when they attacked him, but beyond this there was nothing to help him. The physical pain jolted through him every time the box hit a bump, and each sensation reminded him of the blows he had received. He closed his eyes and struggled to control his terror. The worst of his fears had come true, and now he could only wait to see what unfolded.

As he lay there his mind was filled with the sound of Elder Paisios' voice and he sensed his presence as though he were standing next to him. He could hear the old man praying, pleading with God for Kellan's safety. Without enough strength to raise himself from his back or hope of emerging from this situation alive, Kellan felt peace fill his heart, and just as Father Paisios had found him in the forest, it was as though he was once again reviving him. Kellan had no doubts that this was more than a fantasy and he crossed himself and joined the old man in prayer.

Kellan managed to sleep a little as the box shuddered on, but his thirst was increasing. He rubbed his hand across his face and found his beard was growing thicker. He had been unconscious for a long time and had no idea in which direction he was being taken. The box came to a halt and the sound of shouting stopped. He strained to hear but all was silent outside. There wasn't a sound for nearly an hour when the stillness was broken by the sound of a woman's screaming. It was the unmistakeable cry of another victim and it was accompanied by the bandits' shouting and laughing. The terrible noise continued for some time until only the men's laughter could be heard when the woman's voice had fallen silent.

A door swung open revealing a night filed with fire. For a moment Kellan could see buildings burning but then the doorway filled with men swinging bodies into the box. The fist landed heavily and Kellan recoiled at the loud thump of the head hitting the wall. A second body followed which landed partially over the first. Kellan pulled himself to safety and could now see a half-naked woman being carried by her arms and legs. With similar disregard she was thrown into the box and the door swung shut plunging its occupants into darkness.

From one of the bodies came a guttural groan that sounded inhuman. Kellan crawled to where they lay, trying to identify where the sound came from.

To his surprise it was the woman who was still breathing despite her condition. Kellan tried to reach her but his ribs made it difficult. He held on to her arm and tried to gently pull her free from the other two. Eventually she tumbled loose and Kellan covered her with his coat. He laid his hand across her forehead, she was burning up. He had no water to cool her and so stroked her temples in the hope of soothing her. The sound of her breathing was like a growl, and Kellan felt helpless. He spoke to her, reassuring her that all would be well, but there was no belief behind what he said. The woman made no response to Kellan's efforts and so he rolled back away from them. Their presence only disturbed him further, and he found little rest for the rest of the night.

When Kellan woke it was clearly morning and there was now enough light in the box to see by. Kellan trembled when he saw the woman. Her face was badly beaten and there was blood both around her mouth and on her thighs. He pulled his coat lower out of respect for her but sensed that she was beyond caring about such things. He touched her face and her temperature was still high. She was now emitting a deep moan and Kellan could barely think of the savagery she had endured.

He looked over at the other two and found they were both men. The first had been butchered and must have died quickly, but the second was still breathing. Kellan tried to pull him into a better position but as he did so the man let out a cry of pain.

"Please," the man groaned, "don't, please."

"It's alright," Kellan reassured him, "I'm not going to hurt you."

The man turned his head to look at him and Kellan could see his eyes wet with tears.

"Where am I?"

"I don't know," said Kellan. "They're taking us somewhere. How many of you were there?"

"How many?" The man looked confused by the question, "The whole village. They attacked us without warning. They cut us down, they showed no mercy." He began to sob and Kellan stroked his head.

"Calm yourself, you must stay calm."

"Who else is here?" The man asked.

"I don't know, a man and a woman. He was dead when they put him in and she isn't doing well."

The man turned to see who had been brought. Seeing her he called out "Neema!" but she gave no indication of having heard him. "They raped her, they raped her right there." He began to sob once more and Kellan rolled away. He watched the man in his grief and had no way of reaching him. As he sobbed the man began to cough violently and started to choke. Kellan slid closer and pushed him onto his side. The man vomited a mixture of blood and bile and fell silent. His injuries were severe and under these conditions Kellan knew he wouldn't survive.

Without warning the door opened again and daylight revealed the full extent of the man and woman's injuries. The silhouette of one of the bandits appeared in the doorway and he threw a water bottle into them. The door banged shut and the box juddered as it began to move again. Kellan found the water bottle and crawled over to the woman. He couldn't risk choking her and poured a little over head.

"Take a drink," he called to the man, but there was no answer from him. "Do you want water?" Kellan asked. The man remained silent and Kellan reached over to touch him. There was no sign of breathing and Kellan could find no pulse. He took a swig of water from the bottle and felt a sting from the lacerations inside his throat. He carefully re-corked the bottle and pushed it under his sack to stop it from rolling around.

The water had made no difference to the woman's condition. Kellan took her hand and resumed his attempt to soothe her but it was an act as much for his own benefit as hers. Her survival gave him hope for his sister. Regardless of what they had done to her, the possibility that she might still be alive was no longer a delusion; there was still a possibility of finding her. He pulled himself into an upright position and quietly watched the woman's uneven breathing, every breath was laboured and filled with pain. He took a cloth and wiped her face clean, stroking the hair back and gently dabbing where the skin was bruised. It was hard to tell but she looked young. His pity for her mingled with his memories and he tried to care for her as he hoped someone would do for his sister.

They travelled on for another half day when the box stopped and Kellan heard the shouting and laughing begin again. As the door opened Kellan saw two men standing in the daylight, they reached in and grabbed young girl by her ankles. With a single jerk they pulled her out and the door swung shut. This time there was no scream from her but Kellan could hear them laughing as they defiled her further. He began to cry in anger and desperation and pressed his hands over his ears to shut out what was happening.

The box eventually began to move again but the girl did not return. Kellan banged his fist against the side of the box and heard laughter in response.

Chapter 13

For two more days and nights Kellan lay in the box. The smell of urine and decaying bodies was oppressive in the heat and he found himself constantly brushing away increasing numbers of flies. The door hadn't opened again and Kellan began to wonder if they had forgotten about him.

He had started to move a little more easily and could now climb to his feet to look through the cracks in the wood. What little he could see was unfamiliar but still it helped to be able to see the outside world. Every so often he would catch glimpses of the bandits walking alongside the box, they looked wild and unkempt and he feared they would turn to meet his gaze.

He pulled the two men's bodies to the back of the box and used what he could find to cover them. Even if he had to smell them it was better not to have to look at them. The water was nearly gone and not knowing when he would be given a fresh supply he drank sparingly. He had resigned himself to a brutal death at the end of the journey and worked hard to gain control over his emotions. Most of the time he managed to convince himself he was ready, but then panic would catch him unawares and he would be overcome with fear. He told himself the one thing they could not take from him was dignity in death and he prayed for the strength to face what was to come with courage. After running from the attack on his village, he accepted that this was his chance to make amends for what shamed him, and he was grateful for the time to prepare himself. But still he feared that when the moment came he might lose his nerve despite his resolve and he repeatedly pictured how the scene would look to walk himself through it. He no longer feared death, he believed without doubt that life is eternal, but facing the means of getting from one state to the other was something else. He found comfort in imagining how Father Paisios would deal with what was happening, and knew the old man would retain his composure no matter what. His thoughts turned to the story of Elder Ephraim and the appearance of angels. It had all seemed perfectly real when he'd heard it, but now, here in the hands of the bandits, he dared not hope in such things.

The shouting got louder and Kellan strained to look out at what was happening. He could see the high fence of a city's defences and guessed that the journey was coming to an end. It brought a fresh wave of fear but also a relief that it would soon be over. The sight of the city left him agitated and he sat down to face what was to come. He pushed Elder Ephraim's writings under his shirt and tucked them into his trousers to keep them safe. He prayed fervently and when the box stopped moving he looked at the door, waiting for whoever would come for him. But the door remained shut. The shouting outside got even louder and there was more laughter than ever before. More than an hour passed and Kellan realised of what little importance he must be to them. They were in no hurry to deal with him, his fate didn't matter.

When the door was finally pulled open Kellan was looking out at a town square. It was busy but few people showed any interest in the contents of the box. Kellan raised his hand to protect his eyes from the glaring sunlight. One of the bandits reached to grab his ankles but Kellan pulled his legs to safety. Holding on to the side of the box he got to his feet and bending forward under the low roof he shuffled forwards. The bandit grabbed him roughly by the arm and with tremendous strength yanked him forward so that he landed roughly in the dirt of the square. Kellan's ribs ignited with pain and he let out a cry. Before he could move the bandit was on him again, pulling him to his feet and shoving him in the direction of a door into one of the buildings. Kellan stumbled forwards and as he reached the doorway was kicked in the back and sent sprawling into the shadows. He nearly blanked out from the pain and lay for a few minutes writhing, unaware of anything but the assault on his body. The cloths with Elder Ephraim's writings fell from his shirt and out of curiosity the bandit picked them up. But seeing nothing but dirty rags he laughed and threw them back at Kellan.

As he began to compose himself Kellan realised he was lying on a cold stone floor, and looking up he saw that he was not alone. Sitting against the walls were groups of men, they looked tired and blankly stared at him. Clutching his side Kellan managed to sit up and look around the room at them. They continued to stare at him without interest and Kellan guessed that they were other prisoners. But their lack of response troubled him.

"Where are we?" Kellan asked. His question went unanswered, "Why don't you speak?"

"What is there to say?" The voice came from behind him but Kellan didn't know who it belonged to. He turned and looked at the expressionless faces.

"How long have you been here?" Again there was nothing. Kellan became irritated and got to his feet. There was a small barred window and by standing on a rock that jutted from the uneven wall he managed to raise himself high enough to look out. The view consisted of nothing more than a small patch of sky but Kellan was glad to see it.

He stepped off the stone and inspected the seated men. They were a mixture of ages but all had the same look of hopelessness in their eyes. Kellan wondered about the particular shame that lay behind each man's survival. "Please," Kellan said, "won't any of you talk to me?"

"We're past talking boy." A middle-aged man sat in the corner; he stared down at his feet as he spoke.

Kellan approached him, "How long have you been here?"

"I honestly don't know. Many months. I've lost count." His voice was flat and emotionless.

"Was it bandits?" Kellan asked.

"What do you think? Of course it was bandits you fool."

"What do they keep you here for?" Kellan needed information.

"Work, we're here to work, and then die."

"You mean they'll kill us?"

"Yes, some straight away, others who work hard they let live for a while. No one's been here longer than me." There was now bitterness in his voice and Kellan was wary of asking too much.

"What about the women?"

The man flashed Kellan an angry look, "Work it out for your self."

Kellan stepped away from him and picked up Elder Ephraim's writings. He found a space against the wall and gingerly eased himself against it. There were fifteen of them, dressed in rags and filth from whatever work they were made to do. Kellan knew he was looking at his own future if he stayed here. He tried to calm his mind but it was racing with unanswered questions. He told himself to be patient; that all would be revealed in good time.

He began to retrace the previous few days; he went over every detail carefully trying to piece together clues that might allow him to grasp what was happening. As he remembered the village and his decision to skirt around the hill it occurred to him that he wouldn't have run into the bandits if he had stayed on the road. His desire to be safe was what had put him in danger. But more importantly he knew that if he had followed Father Paisios' instructions he would still be free, heading east. He shook his head at the realisation that he had put his fears before obedience.

He unfolded the pages from Elder Ephraim in the hope of finding some comfort. Despite the gloom of the room the words were clear and distinct.

Treat each moment of trial as a testing of the soul. The storms of the world will uproot trees with shallow roots, but the trees that grow in storms sink their roots even deeper when the winds blow. They do so without complaint, just as we must suffer for a short time with patience and hope in God.

Kellan felt a sense of peace and knew that anything that now befell him was nothing more than he deserved. Why should he expect anything more? He hid the cloths back beneath his shirt and quietly began to pray. The men around him were prisoners, but as he brought them each in turn before God Kellan experienced a freedom no bars or walls could shut in. He was reconciled to his death and anything between then and this moment could not trouble him.

Chapter 14

The first night in captivity brought little sleep. The men lay in the dark listening to the cries of unseen brutality somewhere outside the room. The screams robbed even noble men of their bravery, and few felt the fantasy of courage any more. Kellan managed to snatch a few hours out of sheer exhaustion but it was a broken and unsettled sleep that brought little rest. By the morning he was just one more silent prisoner waiting for whatever would happen next.

The door opened and a few bottles of water in a net sack were thrown into the room. Then men casually moved towards them and took a drink. Kellan waited his turn and when he eventually tasted the water he found it bitter with age. The other men gulped quickly but the taste was too much for Kellan to bear. He took a few sips and passed it on.

A few minutes later the door opened again and Kellan could see a box had been pulled up to the doorway. The men stared moving from the room to the container and as Kellan started to push Elder Ephraim's writings under his shirt the middle aged man said "Leave it, or you'll lose it." Kellan was in two minds but decided to trust him. He pushed the cloths into the corner of the room and joined the others.

Once they were all in the box it moved forward far enough for the door to be swung shut and then the same rocking began as the box moved away. The interior was empty but for the men and they sat where they could. Everyone remained silent for the twenty minutes they were in there and when the box came to a halt the men shuffled out through the opened door into the darkness before them.

Kellan was one of the first out and found himself in an unlit cave. The floor was deep with mud and the air was damp.

"Get on!" A loud voice barked at them and they headed deeper into the darkness before them. Kellan had never been underground before and as the path sloped down the sense of being swallowed by the earth was claustrophobic. A few times he had to push against the wall of the cave to keep his balance in the mud and each time his hand sank into the moist walls that felt dangerously unstable and soft. There were few support beams and it was obvious that at some point the cave would collapse.

The cave opened into a large chamber where oil lamps revealed scarred walls in every direction. A group of bandits were handing out small shovels and picks and pushing the men towards different points at the walls. Without instruction as to what he was digging for Kellan was handed a blunt pick made entirely of hard wood and was pushed to a far wall where he joined men already at work. For a moment Kellan didn't respond, he watched the others to see what was expected and was immediately struck across the top of the shoulders with a long cane. The force of the blow took him by surprise and he dropped to his knees. The man beside him glanced at him and said "Work you fool."

Kellan picked up the tool he had dropped and copied what he saw going on around him, chopping at the rock and clay which fell away in chunks and slabs at his feet. It was clear the men weren't trying to enlarge the chamber; the work was too haphazard for that, they were searching for something.

Kellan's ribs complained as he swung the pick and he was forced to twist his body so that his movements weren't reliant on the damaged part of his body. But this was tiring and not entirely successful, and very quickly he found all strength had left him once more. But the sound of men being caned was sufficient encouragement to keep going and he pushed himself beyond his body's normal capacities.

After a few hours the bandits called out "Drink!" and the men simultaneously dropped their tools and moved quickly to the centre of the chamber. Bottles of water were handed out and the men ignored the stale taste and gulped what they could. Kellan's physical condition overcame his reaction to the water's bitterness and he drank as much as he could swallow. The men were allowed to sit for a few minutes but the same cry of "Work" was bellowed out and the men rushed to their places once more.

Kellan still didn't know what it was they were searching for but twice he saw men holding something up and being surrounded by bandits who took the objects from them. He assumed he would know he had found whatever it was if he came across it, but he didn't care one way or the other, his only concern was to give the impression that he was working hard enough to avoid being caned. But even this level of effort was taking its toll and he knew he wouldn't heal quickly enough to survive this work for too long. Accepting the inevitability of death while sitting still on the journey was very different from the state of mind brought on by heavy labour, and he wasn't prepared to die this way.

After a few more hours that nearly brought Kellan to collapse the men were instructed to "Eat!" Tins were dropped where the men had been given water and once more the tools were dropped at the work face. Kellan found a tin and sat on the floor. He pulled off the lid to find a grey looking stew. He stuck two of his filthy fingers into the cold mush and lifted it to his mouth. It was neither bitter nor sweet, a bland paste that most dogs would walk away from. His impulse was to refuse it, but he knew his body needed every ounce of energy he could find, he lifted the tin to his lips and tilted it towards himself. The contents slid slowly into his mouth and he forced himself to chew. After a few mouthfuls he grabbed a bottle and washed it down. He repeated this until the tin was nearly empty and he could take no more. Pressing the lid back into place he lobbed it back towards the growing pile of empty tins.

He stretched his legs out and lay back to rest. The sound of men eating echoed around the chamber but no one spoke. He was too afraid to close his eyes but still the rest was welcome. They were permitted thirty minutes before the hateful sound of "Work!" was called out and each man overcame his body to stand and resume his labour. Kellan's legs wobbled slightly as he stood and he wondered if he would make it. He could imagine how the bandits would respond if someone collapsed and he willed himself to stay upright.

It was impossible to judge how long they worked; Kellan's mind had lost any capacity to judge minutes let alone hours. But it was a long time and when the call to "Stop!" was announced he felt he could not have lasted much longer. He dropped his tool onto the pile and staggered along the tunnel towards the waiting box. Inside the men lay motionless, a tangle of aching limbs. Kellan closed his eyes and entered a dreaming state of semi-consciousness; the movement of the box rocked him into a half-sleep that was filled with images from the day. The work had been so intensive that even as he rested his muscles seemed to be filled with the memory of digging and he could still see the wall of clay before him.

The door opened to reveal the approaching doorway back into their cell and fists banged on the sides of the box encouraging the occupants to be quick. New bottles of water were waiting for them and the men gratefully quenched their thirst. Elder Ephraim's writings were still where he had left them, and Kellan slumped to the floor near them, relieved that the day was over. He was used to hours in the fields, but this was different, it wasn't just the labour, this work sapped more than muscles. He looked around at the other men; some of the older ones looked near to breaking: at least he was young. As he caught himself thinking this he felt ashamed, knowing that he had allowed his personal struggle to rob him of all compassion. He resisted these instincts and looked with concern at the frailty of some of those around him. There was nothing physical he could do for them, and so he laid back and prayed.

He was woken by shouting. He pulled himself to a seated position to see two bandits hitting one of the men in the room. It was such an unexpected sight that the shock paralysed him. The man was pleading for mercy but the bandits were oblivious to anything but their intent to harm him. They punched and kicked him until he fell to the floor at which they grabbed him and dragged him out. The silence that followed the bang of the door was a disturbed emptiness. The men strained to hear what they could from beyond the cell but there was nothing.

"What's going to happen to him?" Kellan asked but no one answered. As he looked into their faces there was no hint of concern, and only the middle-aged man who had spoken to him before looked back. He shook his head at Kellan and then looked away. The event made Kellan realise that even here they were not safe. They were vulnerable to the violence beyond the locked door and had no where to run. He was too tired to read, but held the cloths of his book tightly, like a man lost on an ocean clinging to a buoy.

Chapter 15

The next two days followed the same pattern. A continuous cycle of labour and recovery. One man collapsed in the chamber and after being dragged away was not seen again: no one had any misconceptions about his fate. On the fourth day the men were lying in their cell when the door opened and a young man was pushed in; he fell forwards and was struck across the backs of his thighs with a heavy stick. His cry of pain evoked the now familiar laughter from the guard as he turned to leave. For a moment no one stirred, but then Kellan moved forward and offered the new arrival a bottle of water.

"Thank you," the young man gasped before taking a drink.

"Are you alright?" Kellan asked.

"I think so, where am I?"

Before Kellan could answer, the middle aged prisoner grabbed Kellan's shoulder and said "Don't!"

"What are you talking about?" Kellan responded.

"Just don't!" The man moved back to his place against the wall.

"It's alright," Kellan tried to assure the young man who looked no more than eighteen, "have some more water."

As Kellan was helping him to his feet the door burst open and in a single action a bandit leaped into the room and struck Kellan across the side of the head with a stick. Kellan was thrown backwards into a group of men lying on the floor who scrambled to get away from him and remove themselves from what was taking place. Kellan landed heavily and was too disorientated by the blow to see what was happening. The bandit hit the youth repeatedly until he began to sob like a child. The beating concluded with a kick to the face that filled the young man's features with blood. The bandit casually strolled from the room and the other prisoners sat staring at the victim of the assault. Kellan pressed his hand against the wound on his head and felt the blood flowing. He looked at his palm and it was covered in red. He couldn't judge how deep the cut was but tried to reassure himself with the knowledge that head wounds always produce a lot of blood. His head throbbed and he knew it was a severe impact, but there was nothing he could do and he knew no one was going to help.

One of the prisoners sitting close to him whispered "It's your own fault; you should have left him alone."

The youth was continuing to cry but this time Kellan didn't respond. Instead he lay clutching his head, waiting for the pain to subside. Streaks of blood slowly dried on his face but Kellan could have no idea about how macabre he looked. He closed his eyes and eventually managed to sleep but through out the night the pain kept waking him. By the time the door opened to a new day of labour his appearance was truly transformed into that of the ghouls he had seen when he first arrived in the cell.

The day progressed exactly like the others but when they sat to eat, a small piece of slate was dropped next to him. Kellan looked up to see the middle-aged man walking away. On the slate were scratched a few words: *Stay silent. Watching us. Escape?* A few seconds late the man again came close to where Kellan was sitting, he knocked the slate from his hand and quickly crushed it beneath his foot before walking off. When the order was given to return to work Kellan exchanged glances with him and nodded his desire to be free.

With a new hope growing inside him the afternoon's work didn't feel as difficult as his mind raced with possibilities. He was already accustomed to the routine of their lives and couldn't see any opportunity for escape. But knowing that someone shared his desire for freedom gave him encouragement. The other man made a point of not looking at Kellan for the rest of the shift and Kellan understood they would have to be patient.

During the first water break the following day Kellan moved to sit beside the man in the hope of exchanging some ideas but as he lowered himself he was greeted with an aggressive shout "Get away, this is my space." Kellan hoped it was a performance for the guards but wondered how long the man was willing to wait before trying to get away.

After ten days of imprisonment nearly a third of the men had been replaced with fresh arrivals. A few had been dragged out during the night but others had either collapsed from exhaustion or an unwillingness to continue. Kellan had begun to wonder if anything was going to come of his hopes when he discovered a new part of the prisoners' routine. Every two weeks the men were allowed to bathe in a pool which had been dug near the centre of the town. When the box appeared at the doorway Kellan had no idea that the day would be different, they entered as normal just as they would for work. But the journey was brief and when the door opened it was clear something unfamiliar was happening. The men who had been prisoners for a long time rushed out of the box into the sunshine and Kellan could hear laughter and shouting. It was a different sound to the usual mockery of the bandits but he could tell it wasn't coming from the prisoners. He edged his way to the entrance to see the men in the pool, the water up to their chests. They were grouped together near the middle of the water and around the edges of the pool were some of the townsfolk shouting and throwing stones at the prisoners.

Kellan considered staying where he was but the sight of one of the bandits heading towards him convinced him to jump into the water. The few who had remained in the box were attacked and beaten, both by the guards and others. The ferocity of the beating was worse than anything Kellan had yet witnessed and it was obvious that some of the prisoners wouldn't survive the onslaught.

He waded out to the others and was struck on the shoulder by a sharp stone. It was a heavy impact which broke the skin and immediately the water around him began to turn crimson. He ducked down under the water and swam the final few yards to the others. When he surfaced the level of noise had risen and even the prisoners were shouting. The chaos of the scene alarmed him and he suspected they were all about to be killed. He scanned the crowd to spot rocks being thrown and managed to avoid being hit again. The middle-aged man pulled him to the middle of the men and began speaking quickly.

"When they take us back they'll get drunk. There's no work today so we're left in the cell. If we can get one of the guards to come in we have a chance."

"But how can we beat them? We're weak, look at us, what chance do we have?" Kellan was disappointed that the man's plan extended to nothing more than trying to overcome a guard.

"If we stay here we'll die. We have no choice. Are you in?"

Kellan's desire to escape was greater than his concern for the plan going wrong. "Alright, yes I'll do it."

The man moved away and Kellan felt a mixture of excitement and fear. But as he looked at the leering faces trying to injure them he was convinced he had to get away. They had been in the water just a few minutes but already a number of the prisoners were bleeding heavily. One man was face down in the water, a growing slick of scarlet around him.

After what felt like a long time the guards instructed the men to get back into the box, but the crowd didn't stop throwing. In response to the men's hesitation to make themselves an easier target by getting closer to the bank three bull dogs were released from the opposite side to cheers from the onlookers. The prisoners scrabbled in their panic to make it back to the container but the dogs were gaining on them quickly. Many in the crowd were drunk and their shots were wild, but as the men came near a few of the crowd managed to hit their targets.

Kellan climbed into the box and looked back at the dogs. They had caught one of the prisoners and even though they were swimming they were managing to maul him. He tried to push them under the water but was overcome and Kellan looked away as one of the bulldogs latched onto the man's throat. Kellan moved to the back of the box, holding his side which was complaining badly.

As the last of the prisoners were pushed in the doors shut and the crowd began banging wildly on the outside. They were out of control and wanting more amusement and Kellan felt a huge relief when the box started moving. The cell seemed a comparative place of safety to this insanity and he realised that the violence of the bandits was typical of the whole town.

Once they were back in their cell the men nursed their wounds and shivered dry. Kellan found his eyes settling on his co-conspirator who never once looked back at him. He retrieved Elder Ephraim's writings and as he had so often done in this place, held them tightly against his chest for comfort.

A few hours later most of the prisoners were sleeping or trying to sleep. Kellan sat with his back against the wall, watching and waiting. His stomach tightened and he kept telling himself that in a short time he would be free again: through his mind went the mantra that he just had to get through whatever lay between then and now. His mind was full of doubts; what if they weren't drunk? What if more than one guard came in? What if the hours of labour had robbed them of too much strength?

He expected the man to start shouting or banging against the door to draw the guard in but to his surprise he simply started muttering. His voice was too low to make out the meaning but it suggested the sound of someone in conversation. He did this for a few minutes, all the time watching the door. Other men began to stir and look across at him; some thought he had lost his mind and many feared for their own safety, knowing how the guards were likely to respond.

The inevitable swing of the door turned every head in the cell as one of the guards stumbled in. He carried his heavy stick over his shoulder and in an action that revealed the prisoners were being watched he headed straight towards the source of the noise. He was moving quickly but didn't anticipate what was coming. Kellan leaped from behind him and managed to pull his forearm tightly up under the guard's chin. The guard roared in anger and tried to throw him off by spinning, but the other man lunged at his legs and was able to topple him. Once he was down the other prisoner began punching the guard in the stomach as Kellan lay under him, still trying to choke him. A third prisoner pulled the stick from his hands and began beating the guard across the face. The sickening thud of the blows only urged him on and in less than a minute the guard lay still.

Kellan released his grip and his arms flopped to the ground, if the guard had fought on for just a little while longer he would have broken free, Kellan had used every bit of his remaining strength.

The middle-aged man clambered to the doorway and looked out into the street. No one was rushing their way, there were a few people milling around not far away but they were too drunk to notice anything out of the ordinary.

He looked back and whispered "Come on lads, we have to get out now."

Kellan pulled himself free from beneath the guard and headed towards the door. But remembering Elder Ephraim's book which had fallen from his shirt he went back to retrieve it.

"Come on," the man hissed at him, "what are you doing?"

Kellan quickly joined him at the doorway, the third fighter too, but the other prisoners sat motionless.

"Why are you just sitting there?" Kellan said. They didn't respond and the three prisoners slipped out into the street. They pushed the door shut behind them and looked around for a direction in which to head. The shadows of a side alley leading off from the square looked a promising place to hide and without breaking into a run they made their way there as quickly as they could. From the buildings they could hear what sounded like parties, but there was an air of menace about them. The laughter was joyless and the conversations were filled with swearing and curses, people everywhere sounded to be on the verge of violence.

In the shadows they gripped one another's arms as though meeting for the first time.

"I'm Unwin," said the middle aged man.

Kellan introduced himself and the third man, a wiry figure about Kellan's age said "Peter".

The two younger men looked at Unwin with a sense of expectation, "Where should we go?" Kellan asked.

"I don't know," said Unwin, "I've never been loose here before."

"We need to find a way through the town walls," said Peter. "The gates will be watched, we need to climb."

The other two agreed, they ran deeper into the shadows of the alley and followed it to the street running parallel to the one from where they had come. From here they could see the town wall down at the far end of the street but there were groups moving around, some of them shouting and all appeared to be drinking.

"We're going to have to bluff our way to the wall," said Peter.

"But how?" Unwin asked, "Look at us; we'll stand out a mile."

"Not in this light, and the way they're drinking we can do it. We just have to hold our nerve and keep going. Try to look like you belong here."

"Okay," Kellan said, "let's do it."

"Why don't we wait a few hours? We can hide here and make a break for it when they're sleeping." Unwin said hesitantly.

"No," said Peter, "once they find the guard they'll be looking for us. We have to go now."

Unwin nodded agreement, but his expression of uncertainty could be seen even in the dark. Peter moved to the edge of the street and looked up and down to assess their chances. "Come on," he whispered, and walked out into the light. The other two followed on, attempting to look as casual as their nerves would allow. They passed a pair of men arguing loudly who paid them no attention. Nearer to the town wall they hid once more in a side street.

Unwin shook his head, "Look at the gate, there's three guards. We'll never get through them even if they're drinking."

The two younger men agreed. "We've got to get out quickly," said Peter, "they'll find that guard soon. It's now or never."

"If you're going to take on the guards you can count me out," said Unwin. "I want to get out, but I'm not throwing my life away without a chance."

Unwin's concerns made good sense and they stood for a moment, the adrenalin still pumping through their bodies making them jittery and Kellan could feel his hands shaking.

"Okay," said Peter "look at that roof." He pointed a little further along the wall to where one of the buildings was positioned closer to it than any of the others. "If we can get up there we can jump across." The three of them calculated the jump and it looked possible.

"Okay," said Unwin, "let's give it a go." They walked out into the main street and got as close to their target as possible. They ducked back behind the structure and started looking for a way up on to the roof. But there was nothing to climb and it seemed that they were stuck.

"We'll have to go through the house," said Peter.

"Are you crazy?" Unwin gazed at the light coming from two of the building's windows. "If anyone catches us in there it's over."

"I can't see any other way," said Kellan as he nodded his agreement to Peter. "But what shall we do if we meet someone?"

"What are you talking about?" Peter said. "It's obvious what we'll have to do."

"What if it's a woman, or a child?" Kellan said.

The other two looked back at him without an answer and Kellan understood what would be done. Peter moved to the door and slowly turned the handle. It was unlocked and he eased it slightly open to listen for anyone behind it. "Come on," he whispered, and disappeared into the house. Unwin followed and turned to Kellan and instructed him to shut the door after he was in.

They were in a dark room but could see light coming from an open doorway where the sound of talking could be heard. The three men slowly made their way through to a hallway where a thin stairway went up into the shadows above them. Peter carefully tested the second step and began climbing. Even moving slowly he was unable to avoid the creaking of wood and the three of them twisted to watch the doorway behind them as they went. Peter was now on the second floor and from the shadows he beckoned them up with a wave of his hand. They were relieved to be away from the occupied room but now found themselves in a hallway so dark they couldn't make out which way to head. They instinctively slid their hands along the wall feeling for a doorway and as their eyes adjusted to the darkness Peter spotted another stairway ahead of them. "Follow me," he whispered and pulled on Unwin's sleeve to guide him forwards.

The second set of stairs was barely more than a permanent ladder and they could see neither light nor an opening above it. Peter slowly climbed to within reaching distance of the top and pressed his fingers against the wooden panel that blocked their route. At first he feared it was locked, but with more pressure he felt it lift. The panel was laid loose without hinges and as Peter pushed with both hands it moved free but tilted from his palms. He had only raised it a few inches but as it fell its weight was enough to cause a loud thump. The three of them froze, listening for signs of response but nothing stirred. Peter slid the panel free from the space above them and climbed up into the next level of the building. He reached down and grabbed hold of Unwin's shoulders and pulled to help the heavier man up. The two of them were doing the same with Kellan when the hallway beneath them lit up.

Kellan scrambled through and the three men searched franticly for a way out. One section of the ceiling sloped steeply to the floor and contained a shutter. As they ran towards it light streamed through the open hatch as someone with an oil lamp began to climb after them. Unwin doubled back and lifted the heavy panel above his head. A man's face emerged through the opening and he lifted the oil lamp to see into the room. Before he could react to the sight of Kellan and Peter standing across from him Unwin swung the panel so that the edge cut down into the man's head. The momentum of the impact threw his entire body backwards and he dropped from sight and landed with a crash without uttering a sound. Unwin looked down at him at the bottom of the steps and it was clear he was dead.

"Put the panel back into position," said Peter, as he began dragging a wooden cupboard towards the hatch. Together the three of them lifted it over the panel as they heard someone shouting in the hallway.

"Quick!" Unwin said unnecessarily as they pushed open the shutter in the ceiling. The night sky was filled with stars above them as they found themselves looking out from the roof at the town below. They climbed through onto the sloping section of roof and with as much haste as possible crawled round onto the flat part of the roof. From here they could see that the wall was much further away than it had looked from the ground and doubts about the jump flooded Unwin's mind. "We'll never make it," he said, "What are we going to do?"

"We've got no choice," said Peter still staring at the gap between them and the wall.

"They know we're here," added Kellan, "we have to jump."

"It's no higher than the roof," said Peter, "we can do it."

Before Unwin could protest any further Peter stepped back from the edge to give himself as much of a run as the roof would allow. He took a few deep breaths and then ran past the other two. As he reached the edge he propelled himself out into open space in an arc towards the wall. He hit it hard but managed to hook his arms over it on impact, his body hanging beneath him. Without hesitation he pulled himself up and over onto the wall and rolled out of sight.

For a few seconds the other two men stood looking for him, unsure where he had gone. But then he reappeared, signalling them to follow him.

"Shall I go next?" Kellan asked.

"Yes," said Unwin, "go on."

Kellan copied Peter's technique; he made the sign of the cross and then rocked himself a few times and then ran as fast as he could before leaping forwards. At the last moment he thought he was going to fall short but as his arms caught the lip of the wall Peter grabbed onto him and held him steady. Kellan climbed to safety and patted Peter's shoulder in relief. They looked across at Unwin who was standing at the very edge of the roof from where he would have to jump.

"I can't make it," he whispered. "I'm sorry."

"Come on," said Kellan, "we'll catch you."

"Do it quickly," said Peter, "come on man, now!"

Unwin moved back to begin his run and was acutely aware of his age and size. He stood motionless, staring ahead of him. Down in the street there was screaming and they knew someone had found the body. It was enough to prompt Unwin into action and he strode quickly across the roof. At the edge he swung his arms and jumped into the night air. It looked as though he would fail to reach his target but as he crashed into the side of the wall Kellan and Peter managed to grab enough of him to prevent him from falling. He reached up and held tightly to Kellan's arm and pulling on him was able to lift his belly onto the wall. He swung his legs up beside him and was helped over the wall's edge by the other two men.

A narrow path ran around the top of the wall with a raised edge either side of it. Lying flat they were now invisible to anyone on the ground both in and outside town despite the bright night. Peter edged his way to look over the other side.

"There's no one there," he whispered, "if we move out of sight from the gate we can drop down." They hurriedly crawled to what seemed a safe distance and poked their heads over to take a look at where they would be landing. It was impossible to choose one place from another in the dark and they had no choice but to trust to luck.

"Lower yourself as far as you can before letting go," Peter instructed them, "it'll reduce the fall." He climbed over the edge and did exactly as he had described. Hanging from his outstretched hands he hesitated a moment, aware that it was still a drop of nearly three floors. And then without warning he let go. He silently vanished from view into the shadows below and they heard him landing heavily before all grew quiet again.

Unwin and Kellan climbed over together and lowered them selves as far as they could. Kellan released his grip and moments later Unwin followed. As he fell Kellan prepared for impact but in the dark it was impossible to judge when it would come. Without warning his feet hit the ground and his legs folded up beneath him. His knees hit him in the chest and the wind was driven from his lungs. His cracked ribs felt as though they were being prised apart and he let out a shout of pain. Peter's hand slipped over his mouth to quieten him and Kellan gripped his wrist as the waves of pain kept shuddering through him.

"You're okay, we made it," Peter told him as Kellan began to take control of himself.

"Breathe deeply," said Peter, "slowly and deeply."

Unwin appeared from the dark, "Come on," he said, "it won't take them long to figure out where we are."

"In a minute," said Peter, "Kellan's winded."

"Is he going to make it?"

"Of course," said Peter, "just give him a minute." He pulled Kellan to his feet, who checked that Elder Ephraim's writings were still under his shirt. "Are you okay?" Peter asked.

"Yes, thank you," Kellan nodded.

"Let's go," Unwin whispered urgently as he started running away from town. Peter and Kellan followed, all the time looking back to see if anyone was following. But no one was in sight and their legs were propelled by the realisation that they were out. The air seemed fresh and clean as they ran through the darkness and despite their fears the three men exchanged grins as they ran.

Chapter 16

They kept moving through the night taking rests when the terrain provided enough cover to hide. The silver moonlight gave the world the appearance of a photographic negative, every shadow was sharply defined and they felt exposed whenever they were in the open. Little was said as they ran, and even when they stopped to catch their breath they listened carefully for sounds in the night. But there was no sign of anyone coming after them and as the hours passed their sense of having escaped grew stronger: and with it the realisation that what they had endured was over.

As they rested amongst some trees Kellan was reassured by hints of daylight on the horizon. "It's nearly light," he announced.

"We need to get going again," said Peter, "I want another day between us and them."

"They roam for miles," said Unwin, "I don't think distance is any certainty of avoiding them."

"I don't know where we are," said Kellan, "I don't know how long I was on the move before the town. Do you recognise this place?"

Peter shook his head, "I was four days in the box."

"I know where we are," said Unwin, "see those hills?" He pointed to a range that looked about thirty or forty miles away. "My village was near them." As he mentioned home they could see a flicker of memory cross his face and the pain it brought him.

"Do you want to head that way?" Peter asked.

Unwin stared into the distance, "No."

Peter looked at Kellan, "What do you want to do?"

"I was heading east; I can't think of where else to go."

"East?" Peter exclaimed, "Why?"

"I'm not sure, someone told me there is a town or city I will find where I can settle."

"I know where you were going," said Unwin.

"What do you mean," asked Kellan. "How can you know? East of here could be anywhere. I have no idea which direction they took me in, I'm lost."

"There's a city I've heard of, in the east, we used to talk about it when I was young. It could be where you were headed. There is a range of hills to the east and it lies just beyond them"

"How do you know?" Kellan said.

"There are stories about it; everyone in this territory has heard them."

"What kind of stories?" Said Peter.

"It's a city full of wealth," Unwin added.

"And the streets are paved with gold I suppose," said Peter.

"But if there's wealth there, do you really think it will be safe from the bandits?" Kellan asked.

"I don't know, but I can't think of anywhere else to head." Unwin glanced at Peter, "Can you come up with a better idea?"

"Yes," said Peter, "we should keep going north, make as much ground as we can and find somewhere safe and out of their reach. If this city is even real we don't know that it hasn't been attacked, and if it hasn't don't you think they're going to be suspicious of us turning up? Why would they risk letting us in with this threat everywhere?" He looked to Kellan for support.

"I'm sorry Peter, I need to head east. If this city is on the way then I'm willing to give it a try, but regardless I'm heading east."

"You'd be mad setting off by yourself," said Unwin. "Stay with us. If the city isn't there we can decide what to do, but let's stay together."

Peter shook his head, "If they find us again it won't make any difference if there's three of us or just one. We can't fight them if they come in numbers." He looked around them for a moment, weighing up his options. "Okay, but if this city turns out to be a children's story you have to listen to sense."

"Watch your tone boy," Unwin snapped back, "if you want to wander off alone then clear off. But you won't last a day if you don't know where you're going."

An uneasy silence fell over the men and Kellan wondered if splitting up might not be the best option. But having company was reassuring and he didn't want to find himself alone and lost. He tried to defuse the tension, "We need to find water. I think we should keep going until we find a road and try and cut east. Maybe we'll come across someone who can give us something to eat."

The sun was now rising and the morning light chased away some of their anxiety. "Let's get going," said Kellan, whatever we do we need to keep moving." There was no argument from the others and they resumed their journey. They walked at a pace that was nearly a trot, new hills far ahead of them giving them a renewed reason to keep going. Their thoughts were no longer just of what lay behind them but they began to imagine and even hope that Unwin's city was a reality.

By midday the hills seemed no nearer and their heads were beginning to suffer the effects of thirst. They crossed an open field and Peter who was ahead of the others began waving enthusiastically for them to catch up. They broke into a run to where Peter was crouching near the edge of the field. As they drew near they could see a farm house nestled in some trees in a shallow valley.

"Look," said Peter in a low voice as he pointed to a well near the building.

"Let's go down," said Kellan, "come on."

"Wait," said Unwin, "we don't know what we're walking in to. One of us should go first; we need to check it out."

"I'll go," said Peter, "stay here. If anything happens come and get me." He stepped through the hedge and headed down towards the farm. Unwin and Kellan watched for signs of life but all was quiet. As Peter drew alongside the house he looked through a small window in the stone wall but couldn't see much in the shadows. He stood motionless for a moment, and then shouted "Hello!"

From behind the house there was the sound of barking as a large grey dog came running towards him. Peter instinctively turned to run but the dog was gaining on him. When it was just a couple of feet away the chain reached the limit of its extension and the animal was halted as the collar yanked it to a stop. It began barking furiously and Peter looked around nervously at what the noise might bring. Kellan and Unwin got to their feet, ready to come to his aid, but still at the edge of the field above the house. Realising the dog could not reach him Peter went over to the well and peered down into its depths. He couldn't tell if there was water at the bottom and so found a chipping on the ground and lobbed it into the shadows. A small splash told him what he wanted to know and he reached for a bucket tied to a length of rope. He quickly lowered it down and felt it make contact with the water. But it floated and no matter how he swung it he couldn't get it to collect anything. He pulled it back up and retied it so that the bucket would lower with one edge tilted down. This time he felt the weight of water filling the bucket and he carefully pulled it back up. The bucket was half filled with clear water and he scooped a handful to taste. From their position of safety Kellan and Unwin watched as Peter lifted the bucket above his head and pour its contents over him self. The sight was too appealing to resist and without a word they began to scramble their way down towards the house.

Seeing them approach the dog shifted its attention away from Peter and they took a long circle out of the dog's reach before joining Peter at the well. He had lifted another bucket of water up and offered it to them. Unwin plunged his hands in and splashed water into his face. Both he and Kellan then drank from their cupped hands and felt their bodies recovering.

"Look at that thing," said Peter about the dog. "It's starving; I wonder how long it's been left here."

"You think the house is deserted?" Kellan asked.

"I don't know," said Peter, "but if anyone is around they must be able to hear all that barking."

"Shall we take a look inside?" Unwin suggested. "There might be food."

Despite his reservations about walking into someone's house the possibility of food was too good to ignore. "Let's have a quick look round first, Peter said, "just in case."

Peter and Kellan walked round to the back of the house while Unwin stood just in front of the barking dog, keeping it sufficiently occupied to allow them safe access. There was a heavy wooden back door and out of instinct Kellan gave it a knock before trying it. He turned the iron ring of a handle but it was locked. Peter gave it a push with his shoulder but it was too solid to attempt breaking through.

"If we use the front door the dog will have us," Peter said, "we're gonna have to break a window."

He found a piece of wood the length of his arm and firmly jabbed the end through the glass. The sound made them both uneasy and Peter used the stick to knock out the remaining pieces of glass from around the frame. Kellan linked his hands for Peter to step into and with little effort he was up and through the window. A few moments later Kellan heard the door being unlocked and it creaked open. Peter was standing there with a large carving Knife: "Look at this," he said proudly.

They were in a kitchen; a large stove filled most of one wall and pans hung from a series of hooks from the one opposite. A table and six chairs sat in the middle of the room and all looked very normal and undisturbed. Peter opened one of the cupboards, "Nothing," he said. Kellan began searching too but any food that had been here was long gone.

Peter opened a door into the rest of the house where they found a room full of wooden boxes in various stages of being packed. "Looks like someone didn't have time to finish," said Kellan as they made their way to the stone steps that jutted from the wall. There were two bedrooms; the first had an iron bed that had been stripped of its linen and the second was empty except for a set of large wooden drawers. The drawers were pulled out and had been emptied of their contents.

"Someone was in a hurry," observed Peter, "I wonder if they got away."

"There's too much stuff left behind," said Unwin who had followed them through the back of the house and was on the landing behind them. "Let's see if there's anything we can use, there might be something we can carry water in."

The three of them went back downstairs and looked for anything worth taking. Kellan found a blanket which he folded and put over his shoulder and Unwin tried to pull a jacket on but it was too tight. "I thought I'd lost some weight in that place," he said, "but this must have belonged to a dwarf." As they delved through the various items Unwin found a small object carefully wrapped in a soft cloth. Unfolding it he held it out in front of himself to assess it and said with a smirk "This must be for you." He casually threw the object towards Kellan who caught it in one hand. Turning it over he discovered it was a small icon of the Mother of God, similar to the one hanging in Father Paisios' cell.

"You can start building your own church now," laughed Unwin. Kellan carefully took a piece of cloth and re-wrapped the painting and slipped it into his chest pocket.

In the kitchen Peter located two glass jars with screw tops and from one of the boxes pulled a leather satchel to carry them in. Satisfied that they had all that was worth carrying they exited through the back door to visit the well once more. The dog greeted their reappearance with a resumption of its barking, and Peter said "We can't leave him like this. He'll starve to death."

"Are you kidding?" Unwin said, "if you try and unhook him he'll have you for breakfast."

"What?" Peter laughed, "It's just a bag of bones."

"He's right," said Kellan, "it's not nice but there's nothing we can do. We can't risk getting bitten on top of everything else."

Without warning Unwin lifted a log from the ground and stepped close to the dog. He lifted the wood high into the air and as Kellan and Peter shouted their objection he smashed it down across the dog's head. The animal dropped to the floor whimpering as Unwin again hit it hard on the head. This time the dog was silent.

"What are you doing?" Peter shouted.

"I wasn't going to leave him to starve, you said yourself that's what would happen." Kellan couldn't find an argument to disagree but Unwin's willingness to meet out violence went further than he could accept.

"Let's get some water and get out of here," said Kellan, "I don't feel safe here."

As they filled the jars Peter said "It isn't burned."

"What do you mean?" Kellan asked.

"Everywhere they attack they burn. This wasn't bandits."

"Maybe they got scared and ran for it," Kellan suggested.

"And there's too much stuff left behind," said Unwin. "They never miss a chance to take what they can."

"And why would they leave the dog?" Peter looked round at the house, "we need to get away from here."

They climbed the slope back to the field and followed the hedge away from the house. As they headed east towards the hills Kellan watched Unwin ahead of him and wondered how much he really trusted him. As they walked in silence Kellan began to inwardly pray but tiredness and uncertainty made it difficult to focus. Despite their lack of conversation the presence of the others made it impossible for him to enter the stillness he had known before, he was too aware of being with them. And so his mind was drawn out from that inner place to the world through which he now walked which seemed to offer only danger and savagery.

Chapter 17

They walked until evening and found a paddock where horses had been kept. It was sheltered and dry and the three men were grateful for an opportunity to rest. Their hunger was sapping them of energy and none of them had the desire to keep going.

Peter found some straw which they spread out for bedding, and they sat together passing the remaining jar of water between them.

"We'll need to refill them pretty soon," said Peter, "I think we should make that our priority tomorrow."

"And how do we do that?" Unwin snapped back. "We either find water or we don't, there's not a lot of prioritising to be done."

"We need to head towards anywhere that looks like it might have water, that's all I'm saying."

"I think we should just keep heading east, make it to the city as quickly as possible." Unwin's tone made it clear he wasn't open to negotiation. "If we come across water then good, but the quicker we get there the quicker we can drink all we want. And not just water either." He grinned at this last comment but Peter was determined to be heard.

"We won't make any city if we don't find water soon. What do you think we should do Kellan?"

Kellan looked at both men, "I'm keen to keep going, if we stay on the road east I think we're bound to find somewhere with food and water.

There must be villages around here. Can you remember much about it Unwin?"

"Not really," he replied. "I only came this way once when I was very young."

"This is ridiculous," Peter said angrily, "we can't base our survival on your childhood memories. You don't even know where we are do you?"

Unwin got to his feet and Peter responded by doing the same. "I'm getting tired of your mouth," shouted Unwin, "you better cut out the wisecracks."

"Or what?" Peter snapped back.

"Or I'll shut your mouth for you boy."

Kellan stood too, "What are you doing? This is ridiculous, haven't we got enough problems without you two making things worse?" But his words did little to calm them and the two men continued to stare at each other.

The moment was broken when they heard something moving amongst the nearby trees. They dropped to the ground and listened to what sounded like many people running through the brush. Suddenly men appeared from the tree line and Kellan knew them straight away to be bandits. As they ran across the end of the paddock more kept coming, all carrying crude weapons. In the twilight the three men managed to conceal themselves and the huge gang poured past the fence next to where the hidden figures lay motionless.

As the last of the bandits ran out of sight along the road Peter dared to take a look back at the trees to see if any more were coming. "I think that's all of them," he said.

"We need to get out of here," whispered Unwin.

"No," said Peter, "they won't come back this way. We're safer here. Let them keep running from us. The longer we stay here the more distance between them and us."

The sight of such a large force made Kellan realise he might be better hiding alone but he couldn't bring himself to say it. "I'll be back in a moment," he said, and walked in a low crouch out of view. Once in private he slumped against a fence post and held his head in his hands. The sight of the bandits had brought back memories not only of his time imprisoned by them but also of the day back at his village. Seeing them running through the trees had awakened that same fear he had felt and he was shocked by the threat of chaos. He tried to calm himself; he prayed and looked up at the stars as they were emerging across the sky. Nothing had changed in the heavens since he last gazed up at them, only the temptations and struggles of his days here on earth. He remembered the icon of the Mother of God they had found in the house and took it out. The image was faded but even through the dull colours he could see the same tenderness he had recognised in the painting that Father Paisios spent so much time kneeling in front of to pray. He asked for her prayers, hoping that she would give to him the same care she showed her Son. Kellan pulled out Elder Ephraim's writings, they looked immaculate, the cloth had taken on the appearance of silk and the ink looked fresh and bright. He read *Do not offer someone bread that is poisoned with jealousy or suspicion.* He couldn't completely connect this with his situation but he knew he should try to encourage trust between the other two men. But as he thought this he heard Unwin threatening Peter once more.

Kellan ran back to them and found Unwin waving his finger at Peter. "You don't own that water; it's as much mine as yours."

"I'm not saying it's mine," insisted Peter, "but you're drinking it too quickly. We've got to save as much as we can. Who knows when we'll be able to refill them?"

"Please," said Kellan, "I can't stay with you if you continue to argue like this. It's too dangerous, you'll give us away."

They fell silent, "I'm sorry," said Peter, "we should stay together. You're right." Unwin said nothing but sat back on the hay. Kellan rolled out his blanket and lay on the most comfortable bed he'd had for a long time. Peter offered Unwin the water jar; he took it and said "Thanks."

Kellan could sense them coming back to their senses, he tried to get them talking in the hope of restoring some normality.

"When we saw the bandits," he said, "it reminded me of when they attacked my village."

"Was that when they captured you?" Peter asked.

"No, I wasn't taken until much later. What about you? How did they capture you?"

Peter let out a sigh as he began to recall the events. "We were going fishing, my brother and I. They came from nowhere, just appeared all around us. My brother was older than me, he started fighting but they ...they killed him there and then. I was taken."

"How far away was your home?" Kellan asked.

"It was four days in the box, there were a dozen of us in there to begin with, but by the time we got to town only three of us survived. Most were too badly beaten to stand a chance."

"Were there any women with you?" Unwin said.

Peter shook his head, "Why do you ask?"

"I had a wife and a daughter. They didn't even make it to the box. They..." Unwin's voice trailed off as he fought back his emotion. Kellan sat looking at him, wanting to say something that could take away Unwin's pain, but there was nothing.

"If I can find my way home I want to see how many are left," said Peter. "There should be someone in the city with a map. Do the people there trade much?"

"I think so," said Unwin, but Peter suspected he didn't know.

"What can you tell us for sure?" said Peter. Kellan hoped the question wouldn't provoke another argument between them but Unwin's temper was now under control.

"My parents told me that there is an astonishing level of wealth there, they trade with almost all the big towns around here which has allowed them to live lives most of us could never dream of."

"We're turning up with empty pockets," said Peter, "why should they help us?"

"It's said that work is available to all who come, the city welcomes anyone willing to work and prosper." Unwin was pleased with his description and hoped it would be enough to give encouragement to the other two.

Peter stuck the knife in the ground beside him and rolled onto his back, "It sounds like a fairy tale," he muttered, "but we haven't got a lot of options."

"I believe there is a place I must find," said Kellan, "it sounds like this might be it"

"It may well be," said Unwin, "What have we got to lose?"

Chapter 18

The following morning brought rain. Dark clouds had blown from the south and the rain fell in impenetrable sheets. It came without warning and the three men grabbed their things and ran for cover beneath the trees where they had seen the bandits emerge. Most of the leaves had fallen from the branches but there were the odd evergreens which offered a little protection. Kellan carefully tried to position his body beneath the covering but it was impossible to stay completely dry. Now slightly separated the men stood silently watching the rain, each lost to his own thoughts.

It was mid-morning before the rain began to lighten and then almost as suddenly as it had begun the clouds moved on and the rain stopped. The smell of the wet ground reminded Kellan of his youth when he had first started work in the fields. Peter walked over to him and asked "You manage to stay dry?"

Kellan smiled back, "Not really, but we'd have been glad of the rain when we were farming."

Unwin came over too, "Are you boys ready to move? We might be able to find water as we go; it's bound to have filled a few ditches."

Making sure they had everything they walked back out to the road and resumed their journey. There were plenty of puddles but none clean enough to drink. But after a while of walking they saw the sky reflecting brightly in a field and leaving the road they found clear water that had settled over hard clay. They carefully filled the glass jars and took a drink: the rainwater tasted good.

Back on the road Peter began asking Unwin more questions about the city, it was clear he had misgivings. Kellan remained within himself, trying hard to pray. The road was reasonably straight and they could sense they were making good progress. Suddenly Peter stopped and held out his hand. He stepped close to the hedge and the other two copied him.

"What is it?" Unwin asked.

"There's someone up ahead, I saw them."

"Bandits?" Kellan asked nervously.

"I don't know, I just saw someone moving on the road."

"How many?" Unwin asked.

"I couldn't tell; what do you want to do?" Peter said.

"Let's get off the road," suggested Kellan. "We can make a decision once we're safe."

Without needing to agree the three men climbed through the hedge and found a flat piece of earth where they could hide. They lay there for a few minutes, waiting nervously for whoever was approaching. Peter gripped the handle of his knife, hoping he wouldn't need it but glad he had it.

Through the hedge they heard someone drawing near. It was clear they were in no great numbers and Unwin risked raising his head to take a look.

"It's okay," he said to the others as he got to his feet.

"What are you doing?" Peter said.

But Unwin was already moving back onto the road and Kellan and Peter sat up to see what was happening. To their relief they discovered a single figure walking down the middle of the road. He was small and bent forwards, his short grey beard a sign of age. He stopped when Unwin appeared in front of him, "Hello," he said, "are you going to rob me?"

Unwin laughed, "No, we were hiding from you."

The old man chuckled, "Yes, I am a danger to any traveller."

Kellan and Peter appeared from the hedge; they smiled at the old man.

"Hello," he said, "two more strapping young men hiding from me I see. I must be more fearsome looking than I realise."

"Where are you heading?" Peter asked.

"Home," the old man said, "I've been collecting dinner."

"Where is your home?" Peter continued.

"Not so far from here, about an hour's walk. Are you hungry?"

"Yes," said Unwin, "we haven't eaten for a long time."

"What! There's so much food all around you, you just need to know where to find it. Let's find somewhere to sit."

"Through here," said Peter, "we were hiding in a nice spot."

"Alright," the old man said, "we'll all hide together."

They spread out on the ground and the old man pulled out small parcels of folded linen. He laid them out and unwrapped them to reveal various roots and berries. He mumbled something they didn't catch and made the sign of the cross over himself. "Help your selves," he said, "it's all good stuff."

Hunger made the meagre collection look like a feast and they began to eat with some enthusiasm.

"Where are you headed?" The old man asked.

The three of them hesitated to answer, but Peter eventually said "Is there a city east of here?"

"A city," the old man said thoughtfully, "you have a long way to travel."

"How far is it?" Unwin asked.

"At least two day's walking," the old man said, "but why do you want to go there?"

"Where else is there to go?" Unwin said.

The old man didn't answer his question, "If I was you I'd think again. You don't want to go to the city; it's not for the likes of you."

"What do you mean?" Peter asked.

"There are other towns you could head for, I don't think the city is where you want to go."

"Why not?" Kellan said.

The old man looked at him, "What are you hoping to find there?"

"I'm not sure," Kellan admitted, "someone told me to head east."

"Yes," the old man smiled, "keep going east, don't stop at the city. I don't think it's for you."

"You said that already," Unwin felt insulted. "Just because we're dressed like this don't assume we don't know how to behave in places like that."

The old man chuckled again, "You are angry, your pride is getting the better of you."

"Watch what you're saying, letting us eat your berries doesn't give you the right to speak like that." Unwin's temper was rising.

"Leave him alone," Peter said, "he didn't mean anything by it."

"I'm going for a piss," Unwin said getting to his feet and walking off.

The old man glanced at Peter's knife tucked into his belt, "What do you need that for?"

"I don't know, maybe it will come in handy," said Peter.

"Throw it away son, no good can come of it."

"What?" Peter had no wish to give up his weapon.

"If you meet them do you think your little knife will save you? If you try and fight with that you'll end up dead. Throw it away, don't trust in such things."

"Have you seen the bandits around?" Kellan asked.

"Yes, but they don't go out much further than this. If you're heading east you'll be out of their range by this evening."

Peter and Kellan threw each other relieved looks on hearing this.

"Listen to me," the old man became serious, "I advise you not to go to the city. There are too many temptations for boys your age." This was no discouragement for Peter but Kellan sensed they should listen.

"I will pray for you boys," he looked intently at Kellan. "Don't be tempted to trade eternal riches for earthly pleasures."

"What earthly pleasures?" Unwin had caught the last few words. "I'm in need of a few of them after all we've been through."

The old man didn't answer; he quietly gathered his linen cloths and the few berries that were left.

"Thank you for the food," said Kellan.

"Don't thank me, it is the Lord Who gives us the bounty, I just take what He offers."

Kellan smiled, it was the kind of thing Father Paisios used to say and he recognised in the old man a similar presence.

They got to their feet and were preparing to say farewell to him when the old man took Kellan's arm and moved close to him. He whispered "Only a fool throws away heavenly reward in pursuit of earthly possessions. Don't let them buy your soul, no matter what price they offer."

Kellan was confused, he stared back as the old man moved away from him and began patting Peter on the shoulder. "Watch what you're doing with that blade son, don't let it get you into trouble."

Finally he turned to Unwin and chuckled, "You're a big man but your patience is so small. Forgive me if I have offended you."

Unwin smiled, "I'm not offended, I can put up with a lot more than you when I've had something to eat."

The old man nodded, "Look out for the shoots and there will be plenty to eat as you go. But don't get greedy; only take as much as you need."

Unwin laughed off the old man's comments and Kellan was relieved that things had become good natured again. They repeated their thanks to him and stepped out into the road. The three of them watched as the old man set off by himself, and Unwin said "Come on, let's get going."

With the possibility of sleeping through a night without the threat of bandits they walked briskly and the old man's confirmation of the city's location raised their spirits. Unwin now felt vindicated, he had begun to doubt his memories but now the others knew he was right. Peter fingered his knife as he walked, unable to give up the little security he could find on the road, and Kellan began to wonder if the fulfilment of Father Paisios' words was coming close.

Chapter 19

Kellan was woken by the screech of a crow. He looked up to see its black shape in the bare branches above him. Its cold eye stared down at him and Kellan couldn't distinguish it from the bird he had seen before. He knew it must be a different one, but it looked exactly the same and its presence struck him as being more than coincidence.

Before he could fully come round he heard Peter shouting "He's taken it!"

Kellan rolled over to see Peter patting the ground around where he had been sleeping.

"What are you looking for?" Kellan asked.

"My knife," shouted Peter, "that thieving bastard has stolen my knife."

"Are you sure it's missing?"

"Yes," insisted Peter, "I stuck it in the ground next to me, it's gone."

"Maybe he just wanted to cut some roots, he could be finding us food."

"I don't care what he's doing," said Peter, "it's mine."

Kellan rubbed the remaining sleep from his eyes and as he was taking a drink from one of the jars Unwin approached from some bushes. In his hand was Peter's knife.

"What are you doing taking my knife?"

"Don't be ridiculous," Unwin said, "I needed it and you were asleep. I didn't want to wake you." He raised his arm to reveal a fist of long roots he had cut loose, "Look what I've found." He seemed to expect appreciation for his efforts.

"To hell with your food," Peter was now moving towards him, "I'll be eating better than that by the end of the day. Give me my knife."

The lack of gratitude for his work annoyed Unwin, he swung the knife out of reach, "Don't grab, boy, it's rude."

Peter responded without thinking, he pushed his flat palms hard into Unwin's chest who lost his balance and fell backwards. Jumping quickly to his feet Unwin charged at the younger man and the two of them crashed to the ground. Peter threw a punch which glanced off the side of Unwin's head. He responded by pulling his head back and smashing his forehead into Peter's face who let out a cry of shock and pain. Unwin followed it up with a back-hand slap that rocked Peter's head back and for a moment left him disorientated. As Unwin climbed to his feet he looked across at Kellan as though to explain himself but before he could speak Peter grabbed the knife which had been dropped as they fell. With all his strength he swung the blade point first up into Unwin's stomach who immediately let out a gasp of surprise and pain as he stumbled backwards the handle of the knife sticking out of him. He took a couple of unsteady steps backwards and fell to his side, groaning as he hit the floor.

Kellan ran towards him, horrified at what he had witnessed. Unwin's shirt was turning dark and bubbles of blood were beginning to appear around his nose and mouth. Kellan went to reach for the knife but pulled back his hand, unable to bring himself to touch it. He pushed his arm under Unwin's neck and leaned close to his face.

"It's alright," he kept repeating, "you're going to be alright."

But Unwin was beginning to make sickening gurgling sounds as the blood escaped within him. Peter moved closer but said nothing; he couldn't tell if Unwin was aware of him.

His eyes focussed on Kellan and he seemed to regain consciousness for a moment.

"Kellan, help me." There was barely any breath behind the words and Kellan could see he was dying. In a low voice Unwin almost groaned "I'm sorry, I..."

"It's alright Unwin, stay calm, don't speak."

"No, please listen, I..."

"Just rest, don't push yourself."

"Listen Kellan, I....I let the bandits take my wife."

"What?" Kellan was confused.

"I let them take her, I hid, I..." His voice trailed off as tears filled his eyes.

"We all feel we shouldn't have survived," Kellan said.

"No, I was glad they found her and not me." Tears poured down his face. "I hid and heard them taking her, I heard her screaming, and I stayed hidden. Do you forgive me?"

"I have nothing to forgive," said Kellan.

"Please, tell me I'm forgiven."

"I can't," Kellan stammered, "who am I to do that?"

Unwin's muscles relaxed and his head tilted back. Kellan could feel life leaving him and suddenly he was holding a corpse. He pulled his arm free and sat back. He looked up at Peter whose face was expressionless; his eyes still fixed on Unwin.

Kellan felt rage filling his chest; he lunged and pushed Peter back off his feet. "You stupid bastard," he screamed. "Why did you have to kill him?"

Peter said nothing; he stared back at him with the same blank look in his face.

"Don't you care what you've done? You've killed him."

"I can see that," Peter's voice was emotionless.

Kellan sat back down next to Unwin's body; the knife handle looked obscene and savage. He took hold of it and slowly pulled it out before throwing it to one side. He pulled up the top of Unwin's unbuttoned outer shirt and began wiping the blood from his face.

"What are you doing?" Peter said coldly, "you think it matters now?"

Kellan ignored him and continued to wipe away the signs of violence.

"He had it coming Kellan, how can you pretend to feel sorry for someone like him?"

"Someone like what? What do you mean?"

"You know exactly what I mean. You've seen how he behaved; he was a bully, always throwing his weight around. And what about the dog? There was no need for it."

"Are you seriously justifying what you've done?" Kellan could still feel his anger under the surface of his words.

"I'm not trying to justify anything. But come on, after all we've seen these past weeks, why are you getting so upset over a man like this?"

"If it wasn't for Unwin," said Kellan, "we'd still be digging in that mine."

"So you're saying I should feel sorry for him because of what he did for us. Is that it?"

"No, don't reduce it to that. He was a man, we knew him: how can you dismiss his death like this?"

"He got what he deserved Kellan, I didn't intend to kill him, but he pushed me."

They fell silent; Peter looked away up the road while Kellan sat on the ground. Eventually Peter said "So what are we going to do now?"

"What do you mean?"

"We're probably a day's walk from the city, if we get going we could be sleeping indoors tonight. What's done is done, we need to get going."

"We can't just leave him for the animals to pick at."

"Well we can't take him with us," said Peter, "are you suggesting we bury him?"

"Yes, we should."

Peter was reluctant to waste any more time but could see that Kellan wasn't going to listen. He didn't want to arrive at the city alone and so decided to go along with it. "Where shall we put him?" Peter asked.

Kellan looked around, "We need somewhere where the earth is soft."

"Let's find somewhere close," Peter said, "he looks heavy."

"Here," said Kellan, kicking at the ground near the hedge, "it's got some cover as well."

Peter picked up the knife and found a good length of branch to cut. He removed the shoots sticking out from it and cut the end into a point. "As good as anything we were using in the mine," he said and thrust it into the soil where Kellan was standing. They broke the surface with the knife and stick and began scraping a hollow in the ground. It was hard going with such inadequate tools but after about twenty minuets they could see a man-sized hole forming. Within an hour they had dug deep enough to satisfy Kellan and they took a rest.

"Do you believe there is life after death?" Peter said.

Kellan looked at him, "I do."

"If there is, how can a man like him live in heaven?"

"Are we any different?" Kellan said.

"I suppose not, but there was something about him, something I thought was...bad."

"You think his eternal soul rests on such judgements as that?" Kellan shook his head.

"No, I'm not saying that, but don't you think he was worse than..." Peter's voice trailed off.

"Us?" Kellan said. "No, we just know how to make people like us better than he did. Or maybe he didn't care. I mean look at you, you had me fooled. I'd never have guessed you'd do what you did."

"I haven't been trying to fool you Kellan, I'm sorry you think that."

"Not just you, I'm no better than him. And if there was no hope for him how could I have any hope for myself?"

"You heard what he said," Peter said. "He gave up his wife to stay alive. Don't tell me you would do that."

"How would we have known anything about that if he hadn't told us? Don't you think there was something noble in the way he shared that?"

"Noble!" Peter scoffed. "He wanted forgiveness, nothing more. He was looking for a way of dumping his guilt before he died; there was nothing noble about that."

"I don't think so; I think he wanted forgiveness because he knew he'd done wrong. I think it was an act of repentance."

"Then why didn't you forgive him? If you thought that, why didn't you say the words and let him have what he wanted?"

"What right have I to grant forgiveness? I'm no priest."

"You say it like it's real," Peter managed to laugh. "You could have just said the words, for his sake. I'm not suggesting it would have changed anything, but for that split second before he died you could have given him release."

"That's not what he was asking for," said Kellan thoughtfully. "He was asking for something I'm only just discovering myself."

Kellan walked over to where they had been sleeping and picked up Unwin's blanket. He lay it out beside the body, "Come and help me get him on to this," he called out. Peter took hold of the legs and they rolled Unwin's body on to the blanket. They pulled one edge up over him and tucked it in tight against his body. Then they folded the other side over and lifted the body into the hole. It wasn't quite long enough and they had to bend his legs to get him in. Seeing his knees bent upwards troubled Kellan and they quickly began pushing the loose soil back into the hole to cover him. Kellan scraped as much as he could back into position and then patted it firm with his hands.

He stood and rubbed the dirt from his fingers, feeling unsure about what they should do next.

"Are you going to say something?" Peter asked.

Kellan made the sign of the cross over himself, "Lord God, forgive Unwin his sins and grant him life in Your Kingdom. Amen."

Peter stood quietly listening, unable to bring himself to add anything. He glanced at the sky and was annoyed to realise how much time had passed. "We need to get going," he said.

Kellan gathered his things and before following Peter out on to the road he looked back at the mound of earth that was now Unwin's grave. It didn't feel as if they had done enough to mark the end of a human life, or at least the end of the life of someone they had known. After witnessing so many deaths recently, he thought it was foolish to imagine this one so different, but despite this he knew it was.

Peter had begun walking ahead of him and Kellan made no effort to catch up. They kept a small distance between them as neither of them wanted the other to start conversation. Kellan watched Peter's back and realised that his knowledge of him was superficial and that he had based his opinion of him on what he had witnessed under unnatural circumstances. He even wondered how safe he was in his company, especially as he had slipped the knife back into his waist band. He tried hard to convince himself that Unwin's death was an unintended action in the middle of a fight, but he wasn't easily convinced.

They walked steadily through the rest of the day. Each time the road climbed a hill they looked out at the scene before them hoping to see the city but were always disappointed. As another day hinted at night they began to accept that they weren't going to make it without sleeping once more outdoors. But then Peter shouted "Look!" Kellan trotted up to where he was standing, pointing out ahead of them. In the distance were the high buildings of a large city. "We've made it," said Peter.

"It's a good four or five hours' walk, it'll be midnight before we get there."

"So let's get moving," Peter said enthusiastically, "Come on!"

"No wait a minute," Kellan insisted, "let's find somewhere to bed down and turn up in the daylight. We don't know how they'll react to strangers appearing out of the dark."

"Yea, you're right. Let's keep going for a little while, "said Peter, "and the first spot we find we'll rest. But we have to make an early start." Kellan agreed and they set off with their destination appearing and disappearing from view as the road followed the contours of the landscape. As the sky grew darker they could see lights appearing all over the city until it looked like a beacon shining brighter than the stars.

Eventually they came to a field that looked sheltered enough under surrounding trees to make a good place to stop. Peter was grinning with excitement as though the incident with Unwin had never happened, but Kellan was still affected by it. As they laid out their blankets Peter pulled the knife from his waist band and the blade flashed in the dark. "You see," he said, "the old man was wrong. It brought me no harm at all."

Chapter 20

The city was surrounded with flat fields and as Kellan and Peter drew closer they could see little effort had been made to cultivate or grow anything. Kellan searched for signs of farming but there was nothing. In the early morning sunshine the white stone of the buildings took on a golden appearance and the two men walked quickly as their excitement grew. They could see three and four storey structures and as they got closer they began to spot people moving around.

The final stretch of road was a straight line of about three quarters of a mile. Ahead of them they could see some kind of gatehouse with uniformed men standing around.

"Get rid of the knife," said Kellan, "it could give the wrong impression."

"Don't be ridiculous," said Peter who at least pushed it inside his rolled blanket.

The gatehouse was more of a check point than a fortification, a fence of no more than four feet stretched out around the city and the three men on duty weren't visibly armed. One of them watched the new arrivals approach and smiled as they got close enough to speak. "Hello, what's you business?"

"What?" Kellan responded, "I'm not sure what you mean."

"What's your purpose for entering the city?"

""We've been travelling," said Peter, "someone recommended we come."

"Do you have a trade?" The uniformed man asked.

"Yes," blurted Peter, "baker."

"Very good," the officer mumbled as he wrote something down on a slip of paper. "Now what are you bringing in?" As he said this he reached up and began patting Kellan's blanket. "What you got inside there?"

"Nothing really," said Kellan, "a picture and some writings."

"Let's have a look," said the official, and Kellan unrolled his belongings out on a long table clearly intended for this purpose. Again the man made notes and once he was satisfied he had seen everything he turned his attention to Peter. Kellan was nervous about how he would react to the knife, but Peter looked relaxed as he rolled his things out for inspection.

The official showed no reaction to the knife and continued to fill out his little form.

"Right gentlemen, here are your receipts."

"You're not taking my knife," said Peter.

"Of course not," laughed the official, "what's yours is yours. Keep these receipts for everything you've brought into the city." He caught Kellan and Peter exchanging a bemused look and said "I know it seems very bureaucratic, it's just the way we do things."

They folded away their things and the officer waved them through. The other two guards had

172

paid them no attention during the whole exchange and Kellan felt himself relaxing. "Be prosperous," the officer shouted after them and they waved their acknowledgement without turning to look back.

The road continued on for a few hundred yards before entering the city and now Kellan and Peter could see the impressive craftsmanship that had gone into constructing the buildings. Nothing had been left plain or unadorned. Artistic carvings gave almost every surface a flamboyance that was a clear sign of wealth and luxury.

They walked beneath a large archway that brought them into a busy square where stalls were selling every kind of goods imaginable. The shoppers were impressively dressed in expensive garments and the two new arrivals were acutely aware of their own poor appearance. But no one seemed to notice, everyone seemed involved in trade of one kind or another and the shouts of bartering came from every direction. Kellan saw a stall laden with pastries which reminded him of his hunger.

"What are we going to do first?" Peter said.

"We need some food, so we need some money."

"You think we can find work?"

"We'll have to," said Kellan, "but we need something sooner than that. We're going to have to sell something."

"I'm not selling my knife," said Peter, "how much do you think we'd get for the blankets?"

"I don't know, let's find out." They looked around and found a stall selling a mixture of various items. "Let's try him," said Kellan.

The stall holder smiled as they approached, "You look like you'll be wanting some new clothes."

"No, we want to sell our blankets."

"I'm sorry," the man shook his head, "I'm only selling, we don't come to buy in the market, you need another part of town."

"Where do we need to go then?" Kellan asked.

But the stallholder dismissed them with a wave of his hand as he attended to a customer who was asking about some of his goods.

"I've got an idea," said Peter, "come on." He led the way to a stall selling bread. He slipped the knife into the waistband at the back of his trousers and unfolded the blanket. Holding it up he called to the stallholder "How much bread would you give us for this?"

A short man frowned back at him, "You're kidding," he said.

"No," said Peter, "we want to trade."

The man glanced over at Kellan, "I'll take both blankets for one loaf."

Kellan knew they were being swindled, but the bread smelt good. "We might be able to get bread and something to wear for both blankets," he said to Peter.

"We'll take it," said Peter ignoring him as he handed his blanket over to the small man who was grinning at the success of his deal. He held out his hand and Kellan reluctantly gave him his blanket.

"I'm not a thief," the stallholder assured them, "pick any loaf you want."

The table was covered in rolls and loaves of different shapes and sizes, and Peter pointed to the largest he could see. Kellan nodded agreement and the little man said "Help your selves."

Peter tore the loaf roughly into halves and offered Kellan his pick. Kellan didn't care which was larger and took the nearer to him. Inside the golden crust the dough had baked white and fluffy, they each took a bite and remembered what good food tasted like. They looked at each other to confirm their pleasure and quickly ate the rest. Peter handed Kellan a nearly empty jar and the water washed the flakes of crust from his mouth. They stood motionless, feeling their bellies which had begun to shrink strain with the food.

"It's good yes?" The little man asked.

Before Kellan could express how he felt Peter said "It's okay, but it needs a little less salt."

The stall keeper laughed, "You'd have to tell my wife that, I don't make it, I only sell the stuff."

"Are you hiring?" Peter asked. "I've worked in a bakery since leaving school. I know what I'm doing."

"Are you serious?" The small man looked interested, "Of course we're hiring. No one wants to work like that these days; does that go for both of you?"

"Yes," said Kellan, "but we'd need to talk about pay."

"Yes, yes, of course," the little man came round from behind his stall. "We can go through that later." He grabbed a couple of rolls, "Take these and head up there," he pointed for them to see. "You'll find a place selling drinks, offer him the bread and he'll take care of you. I've got to clear this lot before I can leave, but I'm usually done quite early. Everyone likes to buy their bread while it's fresh. I'll come and find you."

They gratefully took the rolls and followed his directions. They spotted a stall of barrels and pushed their way through the crowd to get to it. When it was their turn to be served a man in his late fifties said "How can I help you?"

Peter showed him the bread, "What will you give us for these?"

Without explanation the man pulled a half-filled bottle of wine from beneath his counter. Peter gave him the rolls and the man handed over two glasses. There weren't any spare seats at the tables around the stall so Kellan and Peter found some shade behind the stall and sat on the ground. Kellan held the glasses as Peter poured generous amounts of red wine. He placed the empty bottle beside them and took a glass. They carefully brought their glasses together and took a sip. It was heavy and a little rich but the knowledge that they were drinking wine was more important than the reality of its taste. Seeing so many people occupied with the mundane activities of human life was a great comfort, it restored their sense of themselves as civilised beings and the threat of violence could have no place here.

After such a long period of abstinence they could feel the effect of the wine and happily sat allowing the time to drift by. By the time the small man appeared they were ready to move on and were relieved to see him.

"Hello," he said, "I wasn't sure if you'd be here. I thought someone else might have found you first. I'm Jacob, what do I call you?" They introduced themselves and shook hands, "If you follow me I'll take you to meet my wife."

He headed off carrying a large canvas bag that was buckled shut and which they assumed must contain his day's takings, but he didn't have their blankets with him. He quickly led them away from the crowds to a small street of less impressive buildings. Without warning he stopped and opened one of the doors, "Here we are," he said heading inside. Kellan and Peter followed and found themselves in a room containing a long table and three good sized ovens. "This is where the work is done," Jacob announced, "wait here and I'll fetch my wife."

The air was heavy with the sweet smell of baked bread, "Smells like home," said Peter smiling.

"I've never baked a loaf in my life," whispered Kellan.

Peter laughed, "Don't worry; I'll walk you through it. I'll have you baking in no time."

The door through which Jacob had gone opened again and a woman with a severe expression entered. Her black hair was tied back and her pointed features gave her the look of a hawk. "You bakers?"

"Yes," said Peter, "lots of experience."

"I'll be back in a couple of hours, we'll need as many loaves as you can fit into the ovens ready for the evening market." She pointed over at sacks of ingredients, "You'll find everything you need. We'll be upstairs if anything goes wrong. But I'm assuming it won't."

"Nothing will go wrong," said Peter, "thank you for the job."

She turned and left them watching her, Jacob smiled apologetically. "I'll leave you to it gentlemen, if there's anything you need shout up the stairs. There's firewood through there," he pointed to a low door in the wall.

He followed his wife and Peter smiled at Kellan. "Right," he said, "find me a large bowl, and wash your hands."

True to his word Peter knew how to organise the Kitchen so that they were working efficiently. He showed Kellan everything step by step and made it all look easy. Once the first loaves had had time to sit he slipped them into the hot ovens and said "You wait and see what comes out of there." He carefully monitored their progress until he was satisfied he could slide them out onto the waiting wire grids that allowed the air to circulate beneath the bread. A second batch took their place and Kellan was grateful for his skill.

They managed to clean the surfaces before they heard the woman coming back down the stairs. When she saw the hot loaves she looked satisfied without actually smiling or saying anything.

"Okay," she said turning to them, "let's talk money. I'll pay you a fair wage and provide lodgings if you need them. I can provide a loaf per day on top if you want it."

It all sounded reasonable and once they had established what she meant by "fair" they agreed. "We'll need to sign a contract," she continued, "Jacob, fetch me a pen." The little man scurried off as he was told. "Have a read of this," she pulled out two sheets of paper, "I assumed you would agree to my conditions so I already included them." A smile crept across her lips and the two men knew they had been manipulated a little. But the contract was simple and complied with everything they had agreed to and they signed without anxiety.

"Sign both copies, you need to keep one. I presume one copy will be enough for the two of you."

"I don't see why not," said Peter, "so have we started?"

"Yes, we'll count this as a half day," she said, "one of you will have to help Jacob take the bread to market. By the way, I am Mrs. Silverman, my husband will supervise you, but it's me you'll see when it comes to payment or anything else to do with money. Is that understood?"

"Yes of course," Peter said, "thank you."

"Jacob," she barked at her husband. "Show them where things are." With that she turned and left and they heard her feet moving quickly up the stairs.

"Okay, follow me, I'll show you where you're staying." He led them out onto the street and to the rear of the building. There was a small shed attached to the back of the house and Jacob waved them in. There were four bunks squeezed close together and a bucket in the corner. "Your outhouse's there," he said, pointing to another small shed further along towards the end of the yard. You've got about half an hour before we have to go, so have a rest." Satisfied that he had said everything his wife would expect he turned and left.

"This'll do for now," said Peter, "it's better than under a hedge."

"Definitely," said Kellan as he stretched out on one of the beds. "But I can't see any bedding."

"I'll ask him later," Peter assured him. "Let's make the most of what we've got."

They lay staring at the ceiling, happy to be off the road and pleased with themselves for finding work and somewhere to stay so quickly. Work in a bakery was a lot easier than the mines, and the chance to make some money would bring other benefits.

Kellan brushed some flour off Elder Ephraim's writings. The letters now felt embossed, almost as though they were stitched in golden thread. The pages looked fine and delicate and Kellan handled it with great care. He opened to where he had last read to, it said:

The wise man trades all earthly treasures for those eternal. The fool throws away his heavenly reward in pursuit of worldly possessions. But the man who stores up gold only saves up enough to purchase entry into hell. The tightness of our grip on our money purse is mirrored by the grip on our heart: squeezing out every drop of love. Worldly riches lead to heavenly poverty.

Kellan immediately remembered the words of the old man on the road and how similar they sounded to what he now read. He wondered if he had been a monk and Kellan recalled how he had prayed before eating. But this alone couldn't explain how he would give the same warning now coming from Elder Ephraim. He closed the pages and slipped the writings under his bed along with the icon. He rolled on to his back and watched carefully for the movements within his heart: He closed his eyes and gave himself to God's presence.

Chapter 21

Appreciating Peter's work in making the bread Kellan took the first turn at the market. He carried sacks of loaves behind Jacob who was very particular about how they were displayed on the stall. He graded them according to value with the most expensive ones to the back of the table. He explained to Kellan how any goods offered in exchange could only be agreed by him and made it clear that there was a minimum profit they would have to make if Kellan and Peter were going to be worth employing. It all sounded reasonable and Kellan nodded politely as he listened.

Customers showed an immediate interest and it was clear they would have no trouble selling everything. But Kellan was curious as to why everyone he served asked about the price. When they had a free moment he said to Jacob "Are these all new customers?"

"Not at all, some are very familiar faces."

"Then why don't any of them know the price of a loaf?"

"Inflation," said Jacob. "We don't set the price of bread, the bank does."

"The bank? How do you mean?"

"We have a City Bank," explained Jacob. "Each week they publish a pricelist for all goods. We charge whatever the bank determines is the going rate."

"How do they make that calculation?"

"They take into account every factor available, the number of people in the city, the supply of flour, even the number of bakeries at work at any one time. It's all very sensible and scientific."

"I haven't heard of such a system before," admitted Kellan, "it sounds impressive."

"The bank oversees almost every activity in the city; it just guarantees that everyone gets what they deserve. If you are a good businessman you deserve to make a profit."

Kellan couldn't argue with the sentiment and was encouraged by the idea of such a just structure. The customers kept coming and soon they were left with just a few rolls to sell.

"That'll do us for today," said Jacob, "you did well."

They stuffed the remaining bread, money and a couple of items that Jacob had accepted in payment into the large canvas bag that Jacob always had with him and taking one handle each they headed back to the bakery. It was still a great relief to Kellan to be mixing with people again and he enjoyed squeezing through the crowds.

"Is there a church near here?" Kellan asked.

"Not in this part of town," said Jacob. "Are you a praying man?"

"I try to be," Kellan had never described him self in such terms before. "I'd like to visit it."

"I'm sorry Kellan, but you won't have enough money for a while, church is expensive."

"Why? Do they charge entry?"

"Everything has its price Kellan, and the bank has to pay the minister for his work."

"Is there a different church somewhere?"

"A different church?" Jacob was surprised by the question. "There's only the one, it doesn't compete for business."

"I'd still like to see the church some time," said Kellan.

"You can't afford it," said Jacob. "The city has different regions; the church is situated in an expensive part of the city. If you haven't got the money they won't let you near it."

"That's ridiculous," said Kellan.

"No it isn't. Every year the minister has to come up with a new way of worshipping, he puts a lot of time into it. No one wants to pay for the same old stuff year after year, so part of his job is to produce new words to prayers and songs every twelve months. His congregation is huge so he must be doing something right."

They reached the bakery and unloaded everything but the money. Jacob handed Kellan a couple of the rolls, "Take these," he said, "you've earned them."

Back in their room Peter was sleeping and Kellan tried not to wake him. He sat thinking about the day and what Jacob had told him. Peter stirred and said "Everything go okay?"

"Yea, I enjoyed it," said Kellan as he threw the remaining roll over to him. "They're charging a fortune for our bread; if we could start up our own business we'd be rich."

"Maybe," said Peter, "but we don't know how much he's paying for the flour and yeast. We'll play it by ear; let's get our feet under the table before we start setting ourselves up as Mrs. Silverman's rivals." They laughed at the idea, and Peter added "I wouldn't want to get on the wrong side of her."

The following morning Kellan was awake before Jacob came in. He entered unannounced and told them to get ready for work.

"Back to the ovens," said Peter.

"No, not yet," said Jacob, "we have business elsewhere first."

Kellan and Peter quickly dressed and found Jacob waiting for them in the street outside the bakery. "Come on," he called to them, "we need to get a move on."

They followed him through the dark streets, wondering where he was leading them. When they asked him he said "We have to buy ingredients and a few other things."

About twenty minutes later they emerged from the edge of the city to find a small crowd milling around under oil lamps. They circled round to see what was happening and to Kellan's horror he discovered a small group of bandits standing away from the others. They stood behind sacks and piles of different objects.

Grabbing Jacob's arm Kellan said "What's going on?"

"What do you think's going on?" Jacob responded. "We're doing business."

"With bandits?" Kellan couldn't conceal his disgust.

"With anyone," Jacob said, "business is business."

"But you know where this stuff has come from. Don't you care?"

"Listen Kellan, I work hard, I'm a business man. If I don't trade with whoever has the best goods my competitors will. How long do you think I could keep you employed if I started getting high and mighty about who I should or should not trade with?"

"No, that's not a good enough answer," said Kellan as he looked to Peter for support who showed no hint of concern. He shrugged and looked over at what was being sold.

"They murder innocent people to get this stuff. If you didn't buy it they wouldn't do it."

"Keep your voice down Kellan," Jacob was becoming flustered. "This city is a safe place for anyone who wants to come and work here. We trade and make ourselves strong. There's nothing wrong with that."

A man in a tall hat stepped out from the city crowd that fell silent at his appearance. He slowly walked around the bandits' goods making notes as he went. One of the bandit leaders approached him and the two of them discussed what he had been jotting in his book. Eventually they both nodded and shook hands and the man from the city handed his book to another well dressed man.

"The bankers have set a price," whispered Jacob, "now we'll find out how much the flour is going to cost us."

Kellan watched as Jacob joined the crowd pushing forwards to make their purchases. Soon Jacob waved for Kellan and Peter to come and help him and Peter trotted over while Kellan remained rooted to the spot. Peter carried a sack and dropped it at Kellan's feet. "You can carry this one if your conscience will allow it." He then went back and picked up a second that Jacob was pointing to. While he carried it over to Kellan, Jacob continued inspecting other items and asking for confirmation of prices. He slipped something into his pocket and handed payment to one of the bandits.

"Right, let's get back," he said. "Can you manage those sacks?"

"No problem," Peter assured him. "Is there Kellan?"

Kellan reluctantly lifted the flour onto his shoulder, he said nothing as they walked back to the bakery but knew he couldn't accept what was going on and be a part of it.

The rest of the day passed without anything being said about the morning's events. Peter led the way in making the bread and Kellan continued to observe him despite feeling confident he could now make it alone. As he handled the flour he thought of the farmers who had planted and harvested the wheat, he imagined the scene as the bandits had attacked them and here he was making their bread.

By the time they were lying in their beds Kellan knew he had to leave. Whatever the city had to offer he knew it wasn't the place Father Paisios had talked about, and he began to calculate when the best time would be to go. He felt he should give the Silvermans a week's work to cover what they had given him but after that he would set out on the road once more. He suspected Peter would rather stay and in truth he didn't want him to come with him. Since Unwin's death Kellan hadn't felt safe around Peter. It wasn't that he felt personally threatened by him but simply that he saw in him a willingness to act in ways that left him feeling vulnerable.

He decided to keep his plans to himself for a few days and would inform Mr. and Mrs. Silverman that he was leaving when they paid him for his week's work. He closed his eyes and thought of the bandits heading back to their town, their pockets heavy with money from these people. The only way he could find enough peace to sleep was to keep reminding himself that he would soon be leaving.

Chapter 22

It was an easy routine to fit into and life at the bakery gave Kellan time to regain his physical and mental strength. His work at the market stall however, no longer gave him any pleasure and he had begun to see not just the commerce but the people themselves in a different way. But he kept his feelings to himself and was sure no one could guess what he was planning.

The week was finally over and as Peter often pointed out as it got nearer, it was pay day. They completed the first bake as usual but nothing was said about payment. As they were cleaning up Peter said "I'm going to ask them for our money."

"Okay," said Kellan, "I'll back you up."

Peter began knocking on the door to their stairs and they heard footsteps descending. Jacob appeared at the door, "Yes?" He said.

"Mr. Silverman, it's been a full week, we wanted to talk to you about our pay."

"Oh!" He looked troubled, "you need to speak to my wife."

He retreated back up the stairs and a few moments later they heard her coming down. She was carrying her book of accounts which she laid on the table in front of them. Opening to the last page of numbers and notes she said "How are we going to sort this out?"

"Sort what out?" Peter said.

"Payment," she said as she continued to peer into her book of numbers.

"You do have our money?" Kellan asked. Having watched Mr. Silverman carrying his profits from the stall each day he knew they had enough money to pay them.

"Oh, we have plenty of money, but that's not the issue." Mrs. Silverman looked up from her book. "The accounts say you owe us two days' pay."

Kellan and Peter looked at her in disbelief. "What are you talking about?" Kellan said. "How can you say we owe you money?"

"It's all here if you want to have a look for yourselves. Though I must say I'm insulted that you would question my word in this matter. I am scrupulous in my book keeping."

"No that's not the issue," said Kellan. "How can you say we owe you anything after we've worked here for a week? We want our payment and then I'm leaving."

"Leaving! Not before you pay your debts you're not." Mrs. Silverman's tone had taken on an air of threat.

"What are you talking about? We just want our pay. How on earth do you think we owe you anything?" There was no anger in Kellan's voice, only confusion.

"Look here," she pointed at a column of figures. "You received two loaves each day as part of your board. But on the second day the bank set a new price for bread. You knew this; you were selling loaves at the new price on the stall."

"You mean you've been charging us for the bread and didn't tell us it was costing us more than you were paying us?" Kellan stared at the numbers in front of him.

"It's not my responsibility to sort your finances out young man. You should have renegotiated your pay when the prices changed – or stopped eating my bread."

"This is ridiculous," said Kellan, "I want my pay and then I'm leaving this thieving place. You're no better than those bandits you trade with."

"Insulting me won't change anything Kellan, don't blame me because you have no head for business. There isn't another person in this city who'd work for the pay you agreed to: I knew I was dealing with idiots the day my husband brought you home, but I never thought you'd try to get out of paying your debts."

"To hell with this," spat Kellan. "You can keep my pay. I'm leaving." He walked out and went back to the shed to collect his possessions. He stooped to retrieve his things from under the bed and paused to drink some water before leaving. Suddenly the door opened and three men in uniform entered. They were carrying clubs and gave the impression that they were keen to use them.

"Come with us," one of them said.

"Where? What's going on?"

"Just move it," the same man shouted. "We haven't got time to waste on you." He pulled Kellan towards the door and outside pushed him ahead of them in the direction of the street. There the Silvermans were talking to a fourth official who was making notes as he listened to her description of events.

"Not to worry Mrs. Silverman, we'll see to it you get every penny back or he'll get what's coming to him." He looked with contempt as Kellan was dragged towards him. "Right," he bellowed, "bring him."

They marched Kellan through the crowded streets and Kellan made no attempt to struggle. Eventually they came to a large, three-storey building that declared in carved stone over its wide doors that it was the City Bank. From a distance the building resembled some kind of temple but inside there were no images or paintings on the walls only slogans encouraging hard work and prosperity.

On the one wall was a huge banner proclaiming the prices of everything it was possible to buy. Kellan's eye fell to the price of bread and realised how cheaply he and Peter had been working. The officers led him to a high desk where another official sat filling out forms.

"Debtor!" The man who was holding Kellan declared. The official behind the desk cast a quick glance at the accused and then reached for a form.

"Name?" He asked in a monotone voice. When Kellan didn't answer one of the arresting officers poked him in the back with his club. Kellan told them everything they wanted to know, but was surprised that they didn't make reference to the Silvermans or the money that was owed.

"Sit him down, we're busy today, we'll get to him." He continued with his paper work and Kellan was directed towards a row of seats to one side of the room. Two of the officers sat with him, but neither spoke. Kellan watched as various people entered the hall and approached the high desk. With some the official was dismissive and disinterested, while to others he gave complete attention. It didn't take Kellan long to realise that the different responses coincided with the relative appearance of the client: wealthy dress meant everything.

Kellan and the officers sat waiting for nearly three hours. By the time Kellan heard his name called he had watched every level of society come and go.

"Come on," the officer to his right said, "time for you to be sorted out."

They passed through a large oak door into a smaller chamber where Kellan was greeted by the words *"Prosperity is freedom"* in huge letters above a desk where two men were sitting. Kellan was pushed towards a chair facing them and told to sit. The two men continued reading the papers in front of them until one of them looked up and smiled.

"You're new to the city I see, but that's no excuse for ignoring the law."

"I didn't know I was breaking any laws," said Kellan.

"Please don't interrupt me again, my time is very expensive and it will only cost you more if you keep me here longer than is necessary. Mrs. Silverman has provided us with the contract you signed and also a list of everything she gave you. Do you deny that she provided you with bread every day for a week?"

"No I don't," said Kellan.

"Then there's very little else to say. She tells us that she was willing to let you work off your debt to her but instead you threatened to run away. Do you deny this?"

"I wasn't running away, I was leaving because..."

"Yes, yes, I'm sure you believed you had good reasons for your actions, but the law is the law."

"How can you have a law that says I work for someone and end up owing them money? This isn't justice"

"Listen carefully; we have built a great city here where everyone has the opportunity to prosper. The City Bank has brought security to our citizens. The one crime we cannot ignore is unpaid debt. If the bank ignored this then our whole system would fall apart. It's the system that guarantees there's bread in the market; that guarantees jobs for those who are willing to work. The system we have ensures real justice for everyone. Who are you to challenge what we have here?"

"I suppose trading with bandits is just too?"

"We do not have the luxury of obeying the petty sentiments that might intrude on business. What you feel is right or wrong doesn't keep the city fed and clothed. Your justice is cruel, it will leave children starving on the streets, it will neglect the elderly. Our law ensures there is work for everyone. Without the law we are nothing"

He turned to the man sitting next to him and then addressed Kellan once more. "Mrs. Silverman informs us that you may have items that could be bartered for your debt, is this true?"

Kellan hesitated for a moment but then pulled out the icon and Elder Ephraim's writings.

"Bring them here," the official instructed.

"No, I don't wish to give them up."

Without warning one of the uniformed men struck Kellan across the top of his arm. "Do as you're told," he commanded.

Kellan laid his belongings in front of them. "This may be worth something," the official said as he inspected the icon." He beckoned a man standing near the door, "Have this valued." The man took the icon and left the room. The official then picked up Elder Ephraim's writings with the tips of his fingers and without a second look threw them back to Kellan: "You can keep this," he said.

The man returned with the icon and a slip of paper. The official took them and showed the paper to his colleague. "Right," he said, "we'll take the picture." They mumbled something to each other and were clearly making calculations. "How many men were sent to find him? How long have we been here?" With each question fresh figures were added to the sum. Finally the two officials looked back at Kellan.

"For the debt we sentence you to three weeks in debtors' hall. But on account of the picture we'll take one week off. The sentence is two weeks, all debts met." He looked to the uniformed men who jumped forwards and grabbed Kellan once more. A door opened to the side of the room and Kellan was taken down a series of steps. Beneath the bank's court room was a long corridor with about twenty doors leading off on each side. Kellan was led about half way along the corridor and pushed into a bare room that contained no furniture and was barely long enough to lie down in. The door swung shut behind him and he was plunged into semi-darkness.

Chapter 23

Within an hour of being in his new cell a shutter opened in the door and an old man's face appeared.

"Here," he said, "take it." He pushed a glass jar through the hole and Kellan felt water moving around inside it. "How long you in for debtor?"

"Two weeks," said Kellan.

"That's not so bad; you should come out the other side. I've seen plenty make it through longer than that."

"Why, what do you mean?"

"Don't you know how it works son?"

"No, please, what are you saying?"

"You get plenty of water down here, but they don't feed you – unless you've got friends on the outside who can pay for something. But most wouldn't be here if they had friends like that, so most go hungry."

"Two weeks without food!" Kellan didn't want to believe it.

"I've seen folks sent here for much longer than that son, and some don't leave, if you know what I mean."

"They let people starve to death?"

"Only those who don't pay for food. It's all fair. You can't be running up even bigger debts if you're in debtors' hall; that wouldn't make any sense at all." The man laughed at the idea. "You'll be allowed to mix with the others after the first week, just hang on in there, it'll pass quickly enough." He pulled the shutter up and Kellan was back in the dark.

He sat down on the floor with the jar beside him. There was no toilet bucket and he began to imagine what the room would be like in a week. He thought about the last time he had eaten and wished he'd forced a little more down. It was too dark to read but he held Elder Ephraim's writings close to his chest just to feel a connection with him. He began to pray which calmed him, and he thought of the prisoners in the other cells. He prayed for those who were hungry and felt his own hunger diminish.

In the dark he began to see images flash before him, memories of people and places. He thought about his village and though the pain of loss was still there, he no longer felt the terrible guilt that had weighed him down for so long. He even smiled at the memory of his sister scolding him for coming home drunk one night and remembered how there had been such love behind her words.

The cell was warm and there was no pressing danger. He took off his shirt and made a cushion for his head, telling himself that a week wouldn't be so bad. He thought of the preceding weeks and measured off events in sections lasting seven days to get a sense of how quickly he would be set free. But it was a bad idea and he soon found himself revisiting painful experiences. He turned back to prayer and told himself that this was the only way he could get through it.

With no natural light it was difficult to sense the time of day and Kellan quickly lost track of how long he had been there. The old man's visits with the water were irregular and he was often reluctant to talk. Kellan would listen for the sound of him moving up the corridor giving out fresh water. He started counting the number of shutters being opened and was able to tell when a room became vacant. Each time it happened he wondered if the occupant had been released or had collapsed from hunger, but everything was done so quietly that it was impossible to tell.

After a few days Kellan's body was producing very little waste but his urine had become dark and odorous. The smell of the cell was overpowering and it sapped Kellan of his capacity to stay positive. When he had been there for a few days he began to think about Peter and whether he could get a message to him. He was Kellan's only hope of food and he believed his friend would do something to help.

When the old man next appeared at the little window in the door Kellan took the fresh jar and said "Can you take a message to a friend for me? He'll pay for food."

"How much?" The old man said.

"However much he'll pay for, just tell him where I am and what's happening."

"No," the old man grinned, "how much do I get for going to all this trouble?"

"He'll make sure you're compensated, will you do it?"

"Where do I find this friend then?"

"Near the west market, he works in Silverman's bakery, they have a stall. You'll have no difficulty finding it."

The old man thought for a moment, "Okay," he said, "I'll wander over in the morning."

Before Kellan could thank him the shutter went up and Kellan was staring into darkness. He gulped some of the water down trying to fill his belly and for a moment it helped. But he knew if he drank too much he would be filling the cell with urine and the stench was as bad as the hunger. He felt his spirits lifting at the possibility of food, but also because he was making contact with Peter outside the cell. Knowing he was still in touch with the world helped to assure him that he was going to get out, it confirmed that the world was still out there, waiting for his return.

By the following morning Kellan was lying in a half sleep, drifting from waking to sleeping dreams, his mind losing touch with what was real. He was pulled out of it by the sound of shutters opening and closing and he knew the old man was on his way. He stood staring at the hatch, anticipating what would come, but also looking forward to hearing word from Peter.

The hatch dropped down and the old man's familiar face appeared. He stood staring into the cell, saying nothing.

"Did you get me the food?" Kellan whispered.

"Right across the city I went," the old man said. "Found your bakery just like you said. But there ain't no Peter working there, and the people who owns it didn't take kindly to me bringing your name up. A right tongue lashing I got from that woman."

"Peter wasn't there? Did they say where he'd gone?"

"I told you, they wanted nothin' to do with you. Sent me packin' without so much as a crumb."

Kellan's heart sank, "I've got no food?"

"You worked that out did you son? Well here's another surprise. I told you I wanted paying for my time and effort, but I ain't got nothin' for me troubles. So here's the thing debtor, I can't be bothered fillin' all these jars of water you guzzle down."

Kellan could feel himself panicking, "I'll die without water."

"Oh no, we won't let it get to that. Let's just say you better ration it out a bit." The shutter banged into place and Kellan listened as the old man went on along the other cell doors handing out fresh water.

Kellan slumped back onto the floor and banged his fist against the wall. He had no idea how long he'd been here, there was no way to count down the remaining time. Each minute and hour hung around him without context or link to any other. All time became a single sustained moment of hunger and darkness. He could feel his mind being pulled out of shape and knew he had to find a way to get through it. He thought back to the earliest memory he could find and from there moved forwards through his life trying to bring every word, feeling and event that he'd ever experienced to the present with him in his cell. He revisited insignificant moments that he would never have imagined remembering when they occurred, he retraced the paths he followed as a boy, the signs of seasons changing, the features of every face he could recreate before himself; everything that had led to the day he had been thrown into this cell.

The cell door opened and a uniformed man ordered him to his feet. "Follow me," the man said and walked away from the door. Kellan stumbled out into the corridor and shuffled to keep up. "In there," the officer commanded. Kellan imagined he was being moved from cell to cell but he found himself entering a larger room where four other prisoners sat looking at him. The door banged shut without further explanation, but Kellan didn't care. He could never have known the joy he would feel at the sight of other people.

"Hello, I'm Kellan."

An older man in his late fifties nodded and introduced himself. He pointed at the other three and announced who they were. To Kellan's surprise the prisoner at the far end of the room was a young woman called Yolanda. She sat with her knees against her chest and her hair was tied tightly off her face. They all looked emaciated, their cheeks were sunken and dark shadows had formed around their eyes. Kellan realised that this must be the way he now looked.

"Why have they put us in here?" Kellan asked.

"We're final weekers," the older man explained. "This is our reward for making it through. There's water through there if you want it." He pointed to a low arch in the wall and Kellan shuffled through. Not only were there buckets of water but a hole in the stone floor meant he was free of the stench in his cell.

One of the other men shouted through "They give us fresh water every day, go ahead and use some to wash with."

Kellan stripped to his shorts and lifted one of the half-filled buckets. His arms were weak but he managed to get it above his head. He poured a slow trickle into his face and could feel the grime being washed away. But his grip had lost its strength and the bucket tilted over and emptied its entire contents over his head. It was cold but fantastic; he let out a shout of delight and rubbed his face clear with his hands.

When he returned to the other room Yolanda laughed at him, "What a state," she said.

Kellan sat close enough to talk to her, "How long have you been here?"

"I was given four weeks, and I've been in this room for five days."

"Did you manage to get food in?" Kellan asked.

"I had some clothes at the place I was staying, I used them for bread," she said. "What about you?"

"I only got two weeks, so I must have done a week as I'm now here." She didn't respond to him, but Kellan was keen to keep the conversation going. "What will you do when you get out?"

"I don't know," said Yolanda. "Find another job. There's always work if you look around."

"Are you from here, the city I mean?"

"No, I came for work," said Yolanda. "I've only been here six months. I'm judging from the state of your clothes you're a new arrival."

"One week in the city," said Kellan, "and one week in jail."

She laughed at him, "You've obviously got a head for business," she said. "What will you do when you get out?"

"I'm leaving the city; I don't belong in a place like this."

"I would say that's pretty obvious so far," she laughed again. "Where will you go?"

"I'm not sure yet, I just want to get moving."

They fell silent and eventually she went to get herself a drink. When she returned she smiled at Kellan but took a seat on the bench a little further away from him. The others sat staring at the walls, fidgeting and waiting for time to pass. It was a great relief to be in a room that had a lamp burning and Kellan moved under it to read. But his eyes weren't yet ready and the words were a blur. He tucked the writings away in his shirt and accepted that this was his new home for a week.

Over the next couple of days the other men were released and Kellan found himself alone with Yolanda. Conversation became less stilted and they told each other about their pasts and gave each other encouragement when they felt hungry.

"How did you end up in debt?" Kellan asked her.

"I didn't really, I was set up."

"How?" Kellan asked.

"I was working for a merchant who was trading in cloth. I thought I was dong well but he had other ideas. He wanted me to work as a...as a prostitute for him. When I refused he threatened to have me locked up. I told him he was just trying to frighten me into it but he kept making threats. So I left and found another job. But the banking officers turned up and when they brought me to court he gave them receipts he'd forged to show I owed him for my lodgings: I was completely paid up but they wouldn't listen. I had receipts to prove I'd paid but they wouldn't go to my room and find them. He had money and I was nobody. So they put me in here. I ended up a debtor because I wouldn't make myself a whore."

"This is a corrupt city; it corrupts those who live here."

"I know," said Yolanda, "I wish I'd never come. I hate it here."

"Then why don't you leave? You can come with me if you want."

"I don't know," she said, "you're not even sure where you're gong."

"No, but I know it'll be better than this place. What about your home town, why don't we take you back there? I'll see you get back safe."

"I can't go back empty handed," she said. "The whole point in my leaving was to bring back some money."

"Forget all that, what does it matter Yolanda? Go home, start again, swallow your pride and admit it didn't work out. If you stay in this city anything could happen."

"I'll have to think about it," she said. "At least we've got plenty of time for that."

Kellan didn't push her any further. She looked no more than eighteen years old and he couldn't bear the thought of leaving her here when he left the city, but he knew she had to come to her own decision. As he looked at her he realised how vulnerable she was, not just because of her age. There was an innocence to her that he hadn't seen in anyone for a long time. She caught him looking and smiled back, and despite her condition he found himself consciously thinking how pretty she was.

That evening two prisoners were moved in with them and Yolanda seemed to become a little more distant. They could no longer speak feely and Kellan felt frustration at their situation. But it was better than the dark cell and he reminded himself of this whenever he felt too miserable.

Eventually the day arrived when Yolanda was released. In the usual way the door opened and one of the officers pointed to her and said "You're out today."

Without any forethought Kellan got to his feet and rushed towards her before she could leave. He took hold of her and said "Find out when I'm being released. Meet me."

"Alright," she said, and kissed his cheek. "I'll see you soon. Stay strong."

"Be careful Yolanda, remember what they're like."

"Don't worry, I'll be waiting."

Chapter 24

The next few days were difficult to get through. One of the new arrivals was a man in his late sixties. He said he'd been in for three weeks and the lack of food had taken its toll on him. As the days progressed he seemed to visibly weaken and Kellan suspected the worse. When fresh water was brought to the door Kellan tried to plead for someone to help but his begging was ignored. Kellan occupied himself with trying to make the man as comfortable as he could be but eventually he began to drift in and out of consciousness. Kellan couldn't bear the unnecessary cruelty but there was nothing he could do.

The day before Kellan was to be released the man died. There was no great dramatic end to his life, his breathing slowed and became shallower until Kellan was waiting between breaths to see if another would follow. When the last one came and went Kellan sat on the bench at the man's head and looked at yet another corpse. Each death he had been close to had added to the growing impact and now he could take no more. He cried out in anguish as every wound and scream and act of violence that he had witnessed now hit him in a single blow. He shouted "No!" and looked at the ceiling, "How can I know you'll protect me when I see this happen?"

The other prisoner sitting opposite him watched without interest, unable to understand why Kellan was becoming so distressed at the death of a stranger. "He was old, don't let it worry you," he said.

Kellan didn't respond, but sat waiting for the next water delivery. After a couple of hours the hatch opened and Kellan called out from where he was still sitting "He's dead."

The face peered in through the hatch for a moment and then was gone. They could hear him scurrying off down the corridor and a few minutes later the door opened. Two officers entered, picked up the body by the wrists and ankles and unceremoniously carried him out.

When the door shut Kellan moved through the archway for some privacy. He began to silently sob, tears flowed down his cheeks and there was nothing he could do to stop them. He cupped his hands and splashed water into his face to wash away his emotions but he couldn't stem the flow. He pressed his forehead against the wall and allowed the feelings to work through him. Life was so fragile, so permanently close to death; the sense of vitality of youth was an illusion. He was exhausted in every way and the only means he had of facing another moment of existence was to visualise himself walking away from the city. With or without Yolanda, it didn't matter now, so long as he got away. The hypocrisy of the people here was more sickening than the open brutality of the bandits.

When he had composed himself a little he went back into the main room and lay along the bench. There was nothing to do now but stay alive and wait for his release which he knew would come soon.

In fact he had lost track of time and the following day the same disinterested instruction was given to him from the doorway: "You're out, come with me."

Kellan exchanged no more than nods with the other prisoners who were sitting around the room; he weakly got to his feet and followed after the officer. As he made his way down the corridor he knew that behind each of the doors was the suffering of another human being. But his relief at being released prevented him from feeling any real compassion; all he could think of was food and freedom. He had difficulty climbing the stairway back up to the bankers' court room and when he emerged into the chamber he found no one there.

The officer pushed him from behind, "Keep going, all the way to the main door."

The reception area was also empty except for Yolanda sitting on one of the benches near the door. She was dressed in new clothes and looked infinitely healthier than when he had last seen her.

"How are you?" She asked.

"A lot better than I was an hour ago," he smiled. "You look good."

"Thank you," she returned the smile, "hungry?"

"A little peckish," he said, "what have you got in mind?"

She picked up a bag from the floor, "Come on, we'll have a picnic."

She took him to a small patch of grass behind the bank. "Sit down," she said, "I'll serve."

From the bag she pulled out a bottle of wine and a loaf of bread. Beside these she laid pieces of meat wrapped in paper. "Don't eat too much too soon," she warned. "I over-did it when I came out and it hurt."

She broke off some of the bread and tore it open. Laying a piece of meat inside she offered it to Kellan who stared at the wondrous sight before him. "It's like a miracle," he said, and she laughed. Kellan took a bite and slowly chewed, allowing every possible sensation of taste to register its pleasure. She offered him half a glass of wine and he sipped a little, "I've never tasted anything so good in my life," he said.

"It's all I could get," she said. "Not the most luxurious meal in the world."

"No really," insisted Kellan, "thank you, nothing could be better. What have you been doing since you got out?"

"I found work as a seamstress," she said. "It's not well paid but it's enough. What about you? Are you still planning to leave or will you look for work?"

"I'm leaving Yolanda, I can't stay here. Will you come with me?"

"My home is two days' walk; I couldn't ask you to take me."

"If you go that far west you'll be in bandit territory, your town may have been attacked," warned Kellan.

"No, I came west; my town is to the east."

Kellan smiled, "I'm heading east. It won't even be out of my way. Don't stay here, you're safer at home."

She nodded, "Alright, I'll come with you. When are you leaving?"

"I have to visit someone before I go. Do you have things you need to collect?"

"No, I'm wearing everything I possess."

"Alright, when we've eaten we'll head towards the west gate and then cut around the city. I have a friend I want to say good bye to."

Chapter 25

The street outside the bakery was quiet. Kellan looked through the open door and saw two men kneading dough at the table where he and Peter had worked.

"Come with me," he sad to Yolanda as he led her to the back of the building to the shed. He tried the door and it was unlocked, and poking his head in he could see a few personal items lying around two of the beds. He didn't recognise anything and assumed it must all belong to the two new men. He went back to the front of the shop, "Wait here," he told her, "I won't be long."

He walked into the bakery and the older of the two men acknowledged him. "How can I help you?"

"I'm looking for Mr. and Mrs. Silverman, can you let them know I'm here."

"What's the name?"

"Just tell them Kellan's here, they'll know me." There was no flicker of recognition from the man at the mention of Kellan's name and he opened the door to the stairs to call them.

"Mr. Silverman, you have a visitor."

"What?" A voice called back, "at this time of day, who on earth is it?"

"A man called Kellan."

There was no response. "Hello, Mr. Silverman?" The baker called again, "did you here me?"

Still there was silence; the man looked back at Kellan with a confused expression. When he eventually heard someone descending the stairs he smiled and went back to his dough. Mrs. Silverman glared at Kellan as she came in, "What do you want?"

"Hello Mrs. Silverman, I'm looking for Peter."

"He's not here, there's nothing for you here."

"I don't want anything from you; I just want to speak to Peter."

Mr. Silverman joined his wife. "I'm surprised to see you again," he said.

"Can you tell me where to find Peter?" Kellan repeated.

"Try the afternoon market," said Mr. Silverman. "He's normally on one of the stalls."

"Okay, thanks Jacob." Kellan suppressed his desire to say more, he turned and went out to Yolanda.

"Did you speak to your friend?"

"No," said Kellan, "but he might be on the afternoon stalls."

"What's that?" Yolanda said.

"The market works in shifts; in the morning and evening they sell foods, in the afternoon it's livestock. Peter must be working a different trade now."

Kellan showed her the way to the market which had been arranged to allow sheep to be viewed in the middle of the square. "Stay close," said Kellan as he pushed his way through the crowd looking for his friend. It didn't take him long to spot him talking with another man near one of the ramps where the sheep were led out for viewing.

Kellan took Yolanda's hand and pulled her behind him, weaving through the throng until he was close enough for Peter to see him.

"Kellan, how are you doing?"

"Not as well as you it seems," said Kellan looking at his friend's new clothes.

"I'm doing okay, are you looking for work? I can get you a job."

"No, thanks, I'm okay. What happened? How did you get out of the bakery?"

"I paid them off with my knife, found work with a sheep trader the same afternoon. There's plenty of work around if you want it. The city's thriving."

Kellan could hear an enthusiasm in Peter's voice that signalled he intended to stay. "Who's this?" Said Peter smiling at Yolanda.

Kellan introduced them and said "I'm leaving Peter, we both are. We're going today."

"Where will you go?"

"I'm taking Yolanda home, then I'm going to keep heading east."

"You and this east thing," laughed Peter, "I should have guessed." He reached out his hand to shake Kellan's but as they gripped each other Peter grew serious. "Can I speak to you a moment Kellan?"

"Yes, what is it?"

Peter pulled him back towards the sheep pens where no one could overhear them. "Kellan, listen,

I know a lot's happened, but I need to know something."

"What is it?" Peter asked.

"That business with Unwin back on the road, you won't tell anyone will you?"

Kellan looked at him with disappointment, "No, don't worry, I won't say a word."

"Thank you, I just needed to hear that. I'm sorry; it's been going round my mind. I just needed to be sure."

Kellan nodded and walked back to Yolanda, "Come on, we need to go."

"Is that all you've got for the road?" Peter asked, looking down at Yolanda's bag. "Wait a minute."

Kellan disappeared into an office and brought out a water flask. "Fill it up before you go."

Yolanda took it and thanked him and they headed towards the city gate. Kellan felt relief as they walked out onto the road and headed towards the customs office. It was like being set free a second time that day. They approached the officers and prepared to say farewell to the last contact with the city when the man in uniform said "Let's se your receipts."

"Receipts for what?" Kellan said.

"Everything," the officer replied, "you can't leave the city with anything unless you have a receipt."

"We've only been here a short while," Kellan explained. "We have nothing much more than we arrived with."

"You must have been issued with receipts on entry for everything you had with you, just show us them."

"I haven't got it," said Kellan, "I can't remember what I did with it."

"I've got all mine," said Yolanda who reached into her bag for the slips of paper. The officer looked the receipts over, "I'm sorry but the water flask isn't here. You'll have to leave it or go back and get the receipt."

"Give it to him," Kellan said bitterly, "let's just get away."

Two other officers joined them and stood quietly watching what was happening.

"Alright," the officer said, "you can leave." He waved Yolanda through. She stepped out from under the structure and waited for Kellan.

"What are you wanting to do then sir?" The officer said.

"Just let me through, I've got nothing from the city."

"Including receipts," smirked the officer. "It's up to you, you can either go back like I said, and find your receipts, or leave everything here."

"Do you mean my clothes?"

"Everything," he repeated, and the two others moved closer, clubs in hand.

Kellan looked at Yolanda for a moment and then unbuttoned his shirt. Beneath it was Elder Ephraim's writings which he placed on the ground behind him. He kicked off his boots but hesitated before unbuttoning his trousers and slipping them off.

"And your shorts, don't be shy."

Kellan took off his shorts and held his hands over his crotch.

"What about that?" One of the other officers pushed past Kellan and picked up Elder Ephraim's writings.

"Please, I can't leave that behind," said Kellan, "it's very important to me."

"What, this?" The officer waved the cloths around to make his point, "They must be valuable then."

"Only to me, please, I can't leave them behind."

"No receipt, no removal. Rules are rules sir; we all have to obey the law."

"Yolanda," Kellan said, "have you got anything you can give in exchange."

She lifted up her bag, "How about this?"

"You're kidding aren't you," the first officer said, "an old bag for something as precious as this." The other officers laughed.

"What about her jacket?" One of them suggested

Yolanda had watched how Kellan had cherished Elder Ephraim's writings while they were in the prison and she could now see his distress.

"Alright, take it," she said, slipping it off and throwing it angrily towards them.

"That's never enough for something like this," the officer grinned, "your shirt too."

"No," shouted Kellan, "you've got her jacket, leave it at that." One of the officers snapped his club across the side of Kellan's face. He clutched his head, "Don't do it Yolanda, they have your jacket."

The officer kicked him while he was still bent over and Kellan went sprawling to the ground. Yolanda shrieked, "Please, stop, that's enough."

"The shirt, or the price will get higher," the guard growled.

Yolanda took off her shirt and threw it to them, covering herself with her arms. She began to cry out of fear and anger.

"What about him?" One of the other officers said. "If she wants him she needs to pay us for carrying him through customs."

"What?" Yolanda, said. "Just let him go, please, you've done enough."

"It's very simple little girl," the main officer was back in control, "if you want him brought out of the city the price will be your skirt and everything else."

Yolanda turned her back to them and walked a few steps away. She let out a groan of anger, knowing that there was no one who could come to their aid. One of the guards kicked Kellan who cried in pain.

"The longer you make us wait, the more upset we're going to get over this thing lying in our office. The price might go even higher; perhaps you'd be prepared to pay in other ways"

"Alright!" Yolanda shouted. She pulled off her shoes, and then after hesitating, in a quick, single action pulled down her skirt and turned herself away from the guards. They clapped and hooted, and as he laughed the first guard said "You see how much trouble it causes when people forget their paperwork?" He grabbed Kellan's arms and dragged him over to where Yolanda was standing.

"Very nice," he leered at her. "Now get going, and take this worthless piece of crap away from our city." He glared as he spoke and all humour left his face as he threw Elder Ephraim's writings at Kellan. Yolanda ignored their nakedness and pulled Kellan to his feet. He groaned again and she pulled his arm over her shoulder. As they began walking away she held the cloths over herself for what little dignity she could find and her efforts were met with more jeers and laughter.

Chapter 26

The further they walked the less embarrassed Yolanda became. Kellan was leaning on her and his breathing was laboured. She could see new dark bruises where he had been kicked but also yellowing older ones that told something of his recent experiences.

"My eye is blurred," he told her, "I feel dizzy."

They made it as far as a small wood and since the clouds were growing dark and threatening Yolanda thought it best to find some shelter. Stepping out of the wind brought some relief but she knew that if it rained Kellan's health could get worse. Yolanda hadn't fully recovered from her time in prison but she was aware of how little food he had had since being released. She led him to an area of undergrowth where she hoped to find cover and sitting him down she pulled at the grass and branches to make it as comfortable as she could.

"Come on, lie here, you need to rest."

He crawled under and she followed him. Just then raindrops started finding their way through the leafless branches of the trees and the two of them lay listening to the sound of the impact on the woodland floor. Yolanda shivered a violent shake that rattled her teeth. Without saying anything she slid up against Kellan and pressed her back against his, each of them with their legs curled tightly up in front of them. But the cold air still found them and a few minutes later she turned and held on to him, sharing what warmth they had left in their bodies. Kellan felt her pressed up against him and welcomed the human contact. He pulled her arms into his chest and felt her fingers against his skin.

The rain clouds seemed to bring evening early but Kellan and Yolanda managed to sleep. By the morning when Kellan woke he was turned towards her, holding her close. She felt small in his arms, her fragile bones barely covered in flesh. Despite their nakedness he felt no desire for her; it was as though she was dressed in something more precious than clothes. His vision was restored and his head felt clear and as he lay there he tried to calculate the time. At that moment her eyes flashed open and she pulled away slightly.

"Are you alright?" She whispered.

"Yes, good, thank you, hungry as a bear, but I'm okay."

"I'm freezing, I can't believe we survived the night."

Kellan felt concern for her, "We need to find some clothes, this is ridiculous."

"There's a farm about a half day's walk from here, we passed it when we first came to the city," said Yolanda. "It's just off the main road, we could try there."

"Sounds promising," said Kellan, "stay here and I'll find something to eat." He carefully dislodged himself and left her under the bushes. He wandered with his eyes fixed to the ground until he found the leaves he was looking for. He broke off a branch from a tree and dug up the roots of the plant.

Brushing off the soil on the wet grass he inspected his find. It looked a little young but when he bit off the end he was rewarded with the sweet taste he was hoping for. He found a few more and wiped them all clean. Yolanda was now sitting with her legs sticking out from the brush reading Father Ephraim's words.

"Here you go," said Kellan, "try this."

She took a small taste and said "It's good, thank you."

Kellan sat beside her and divided his find between them. As they ate Yolanda looked at the writings and said "Why is this so important to you?"

"I'm sorry you had to give up what you did for them," said Kellan.

"No, I'm not saying that," she assured him, "I just wondered why this means what it does to you."

Kellan looked down at them, he had never talked to anyone about them and wasn't sure he could give an answer that would satisfy her: particularly after what they had cost her. He told her about Father Paisios and tried to convey the holiness of his presence. He recounted how he had met him but didn't include anything about what he had said before Kellan left. Yolanda listened carefully, nodding her understanding at certain details. When Kellan finished speaking she said "My family are all Christian. We have a church near our house and a good minister."

"I didn't attend church much before meeting Father Paisios," Kellan admitted, "I'd like to see it."

She handed him the writings, "The cloth is very beautiful," she remarked.

He smiled at her comment and said "It took me a long time to see that."

They finished the roots and headed back to the road. Where once Kellan had listened out for bandits his only concern now was meeting someone who would see their nakedness. Despite the aches in his back where he had been kicked they made good progress and Yolanda began to point out features in the countryside that she recognised. He could hear her excitement as she began to sense home coming closer and he wondered how her family would react to them turning up this way: he knew they had to find clothes.

Around midday Yolanda's prediction was proved true and they could see a column of smoke rising from some trees about a quarter of a mile from the road. "That's the farm," she said. "What shall we say?"

"I think you better get out of view, I'll go over and talk to them."

She agreed and so he strode along the last stretch of lane leading up to the farm house alone. The smoke was billowing from a large chimney at one end of the building and it hinted at a warmth Kellan longed for. He knocked on the door and stepped back to await the occupant's reaction. The door opened and an old woman appeared. As soon as she saw Kellan she began to cackle, "Well goodness me," she laughed, "didn't you forget something this morning son?"

Her laughter was a relief to Kellan but he felt himself growing uncomfortable as he stood in her yard, covering himself as best he could.

"I'm sorry," he said. "Our clothes were stolen."

"There's more than one of you naked boys is there?" She looked around trying to spot anyone who might be hiding.

"No, my friend is a woman; she's waiting a little further back. I didn't know who would be here."

The woman's laughter started up again, "Wait a minute," she said and went back inside. She re-appeared holding a couple of heavy coats. "Put this on and give this one to your friend. Bring the poor girl in for goodness sake before she catches her death out there." Kellan took the coat and buttoned away his embarrassment. She threw the second garment to him. "Thank you," he said, "I'll be just a minute."

He ran back to Yolanda and realised that it felt very different with only one of them being naked. "Here you are," he said, turning his back while she put it on.

"What did they say?" Yolanda asked.

"It's an old woman, she's invited us down."

"Is it safe?"

"I think so; I didn't see anyone else around."

They walked together back to the farm and the door opened to greet them.

"Come on in," the woman grinned, "you look like you need feeding as well."

They were in a large kitchen, a room that occupied the entire downstairs. A primitive set of stone steps led up to the second floor. The room was warm and the old woman told them to sit at the table away from the door. They watched her spooning a thick vegetable stew into two bowls, steam rising as she did so.

"You look a bit more decent now," she said, "I couldn't have a naked young man eating at my table. What would my husband have thought?"

Her good humour raised their spirits and they thankfully ate her food. As they did so she chatted on, a constant stream of observations that brought her amusement. She talked about her chickens and the pig she was keeping, about how she used to grow potatoes and tomatoes and every other garden vegetable she could think of.

Kellan leaned back in his chair, "Is your husband still alive?"

"No, he's been gone four years now. I just produce enough to get by. Maybe one more winter and I won't have to bother anymore."

"Why do you say that?" Yolanda asked her.

"I'm sick," she said, "I've felt it coming for a while. But I don't mind."

"Why don't you come with us to my town, there are doctors there."

"No, I'm happy to die where we lived together for so many years. I want to die in my own home, that's all I want now." She could see them feeling

226

unsure of what to say. "I'm glad his coat is going to a good home," she said to lighten the mood. "It's a good fit."

"Thank you," said Kellan. "Is there any job I can do before we leave?"

"No, nothing, I may be old but I can still look after myself." She looked at Yolanda, "You need a bath before you go, get some warmth back in you." She looked back at Kellan, "Was it bandits that robbed you? No it can't have been," she said answering her own question. "They'd have slit your throats."

"We've come from the city," said Kellan.

The old woman tutted, "They swindled us as well. I won't do business with them ever again."

Yolanda bathed first and Kellan eased himself into the water after her. The old woman added kettles of boiling water even while Kellan was in the bath saying "Don't worry yourself, I've already seen you in your birthday suit and it ain't nothing to alarm a woman who was married for fifty years."

It was late afternoon by the time they were dry and sitting once more at her table wearing more comfortable clothing she had found for them.

"You'll never get home before night fall," she said. "Stay the night and you can leave in the morning. No sense spending another night out in the cold when there's a dry bed that's empty."

They thanked her and accepted the offer. She fed them again that evening and as Kellan relaxed by the fire he watched the two women talking. Only now did he begin to acknowledge to himself Yolanda's physical beauty and he caught himself wondering where they would be sleeping. As the thoughts filled his mind he felt the effects of lust inflame him and realised that he was looking at her with something of the same attitude that the city officers had had at the customs gate. After bearing the cold and hunger together in complete nakedness it was in the warmth and comfort of the farm house that he permitted his flesh to stir these things within him. He looked away from her and tried to overcome the impulse. He did not want to see her as a way of gratifying his own desires; he knew it was a betrayal of her trust.

He was relieved to discover that the old woman gave them beds in different rooms. Lying in fresh sheets with a soft pillow beneath him Kellan felt the tension in his muscles leaving him. He had eaten too much food and though it was a little uncomfortable it added to his sense of relief. He opened Elder Ephraim's writings and without sitting up read: *He who loves God loves his fellow man because he loves the image of God within him. If a man hates his neighbour but claims to love God he is a liar or deludes himself or is deluded by the demons who rule his heart.*

Kellan understood that the lust he had felt for Yolanda was really no different to hating her: both were a failure to love the image of God within her. He began to pray but was tired and didn't focus for long. While the wind and rain beat at the window Kellan slept deeply.

He woke to the sound of Yolanda and the woman talking. Their voices kept breaking into laughter and he smiled to hear them so happy. He dressed and went down stairs and found them sitting at the table. Yolanda gave him a broad smile.

"Here he is," said the old woman, "sleeping beauty is up."

"I can't remember the last time I slept so well," said Kellan. "It was a horrible night outside, I'm glad we weren't out there."

The old woman served him eggs and the two women watched him eat. She then brought all of them hot tea, "You'll be making a start soon then?" She asked.

"Yes," said Yolanda, "we'll be there before nightfall. You've been so kind, I don't want to leave, but we should give ourselves a whole day to make sure."

"Yes, I understand," said the old woman. "But before you go will you do me a little job?"

"Of course, what is it?" Yolanda asked.

"Along the lane I have some potatoes, would you go and pull me a few up?"

Yolanda, got to her feet, "No problem. How many do you want?"

"Just enough for a couple of days, see how big they are."

Yolanda pulled on her new coat and left them alone. The old woman gazed at Kellan.

"She's a good girl Kellan, you could do worse."

Kellan blushed at her directness, he didn't know what to say.

"What are you running from?" She said.

"I'm not running from anything," said Kellan. "I don't want to go back to where the bandits are around, but I'm not running."

"Yes, yes, I know about the bandits. But there's something else isn't there, something you're not saying." She looked intently at him and he felt himself under examination.

"There are things in my past that I don't want to think about, but I'm making this journey for other reasons."

"Yolanda told me about the monk you were with," she said. "Did it ever cross your mind that what you are looking for isn't a place? It could be a person."

"I wondered that myself," admitted Kellan, "but I don't know. There are things I'm not sure about yet."

"Don't expect to be able to answer everything Kellan, some things will always be a mystery."

"Yes, I know that, but I'm not clear about my feelings for Yolanda; I haven't felt like this for a while. I don't know where it fits in everything."

"Do what you can," she said, "and leave everything else to God. What you cannot do God will complete. You're not responsible for the whole world Kellan."

"No, but I am responsible for my soul."

"To an extent that's true. You are responsible for your actions, for your choices. But ultimately you must place even your soul into God's hands. If you trust in God enough you can make Him responsible for you."

Kellan thought for a moment, he wasn't sure about her advice. He was about to question her when Yolanda returned with the potatoes.

"Thank you my dear, put them over there," she pointed to a small table.

They got to their feet, and Kellan found the coat she had given him. "Thank you," he said.

Yolanda put her arms around the old woman and kissed her.

"Remember everything I told you," the old woman said to her. "All will be well."

She walked them to the door and watched them walking away. Each time Yolanda turned to look back the old woman gave a little wave.

"Do you think she'll be alright by herself there?" Yolanda said.

"It's what she wants," said Kellan, "I think she knows what she's doing.

As they walked Yolanda came close to him and without saying anything slipped her fingers between his. He gently squeezed them and they continued walking holding hands.

Chapter 27

It was late afternoon when Yolanda stopped and turned to Kellan. "We'll be there in an hour," she said. "I need to say something."

"I thought you had something on your mind," said Kellan.

"First, it's my father. He's a very serious man, but you mustn't take this for unfriendliness, don't be put off by his manner."

"Okay," Kellan smiled. "You've got me worried now."

"No, please don't. He's a good man, he just doesn't show his feelings very well."

"Don't worry Yolanda, I think I can cope with him."

"There's something else." She paused for a moment. "Whatever you say, don't tell him we were naked for the night."

Kellan laughed, "Are you serious? Alright, I'll keep it a secret."

"He wouldn't believe the way it was," she said. "And even if he did I'm not sure he'd approve anyway."

"Anything else you want to warn me about this town of yours?"

"No, really, I know it sounds silly."

"No it doesn't Yolanda, I understand your concerns. Don't worry, it will be alright."

As he stroked her arm to reassure her she moved close and kissed him. They embraced and as Kellan

232

pulled her into him the smell of her hair filled his face. They stood like this for a few minutes and Kellan said "We should get going; we can't stay here all day."

They continued to link hands as they walked and Kellan thought about the old lady's questions. Maybe she was right and what Father Paisios had seen in the future for him was a life with Yolanda. But there were still too many doubts in his mind to be sure and though he could sense his feelings for her growing stronger he wasn't yet convinced that he had reached his destination. This troubled him because he didn't want to raise false expectations in Yolanda for what might become of them. But the joy in her kiss was powerful and even the touch of her hand was more intimate than he could ever have imagined.

They followed the road as it headed down into a flat valley between low hills. As she first caught sight of home she excitedly pointed out buildings she knew. It was immediately obvious to Kellan that what she had described as a town was really a village no larger than the one he had grown up in. But this was a welcome realisation as he had had enough of larger towns to last him a life time: the more different it was from the city the better.

As they approached the outskirts of the village Yolanda let go of his hand but Kellan took no offence at this. He was grateful not to have to explain too much to her father too soon.

The village was tidy and it was clear that the occupants took care of it. The houses were old but well built and in good order and as they walked through the streets a few people acknowledged them as they passed. A large middle-aged woman came out from one of the houses and cried "Yolanda!" She ran out into the street and they hugged enthusiastically.

"How are you?" The woman asked.

"Good, good," said Yolanda, "How has everyone been?"

The woman began recounting stories about various people, all the time with her arm around Yolanda's shoulder.

"What about my father?"

"He's well, he'll be so happy you're back Yolanda, he's missed you." At that point the woman looked at Kellan for the first time. Yolanda introduced them and they shook hands.

"I have to get back to my jobs," said the woman, "you must come and see me once you're settled."

"I will, I promise," said Yolanda. "It's so good to see you again."

The woman kissed her cheek once more and returned to her house smiling. Kellan was encouraged to see Yolanda amongst people to whom she belonged and it all relaxed him a little.

"Our house is up here," Yolanda pointed to a side street. The houses were modest but comfortable and were an indication of neither great wealth nor poverty. They stopped outside one that to him looked no different from any other and she opened the large gate to the yard. "Come on in," she said.

234

Kellan was nervous but didn't really know why. He followed her to the front door and watched her open it and let them in. The interior was quite plain but clean and welcoming. As Kellan closed the door behind them Yolanda shouted "Father, are you there?" There was no reply. "He must be working," she said, "come through and I'll make us some tea."

Kellan took a seat that was offered him and watched her retrieving everything from the cupboards. "Are you hungry?" She asked.

"No, I'm fine," he said. "I don't think we should help ourselves until he comes home. It won't look good if he comes in and finds me eating his food."

Yolanda laughed at this. "Alright," she said, "I'll prepare something for all of us and we'll eat together when he's back."

Kellan sipped at his tea and watched her busy herself with making dinner. At her insistence he played no part and was happy to relax. She made the odd remark as she worked but other than that there was little conversation between them and Kellan realised that he wasn't the only one feeling nervous.

A couple of hours later they heard her father coming through the front door. Yolanda was now sitting with Kellan at the table and she rushed through the house to meet him. Kellan stood, unsure of what he should do with himself. He could hear their muffled voices as they got nearer and at the sound of his name being mentioned he heard them stop moving. Her father said something in a low voice and the sound of her voice as she answered made it clear they had grown serious. After a brief conversation they entered the kitchen and Kellan saw a man in his late forties who carried the grime in his face of a day spent working.

He looked Kellan in the eye but did not say anything and the expression in his face revealed no sign of welcome.

"Hello," said Kellan, "Yolanda's told me a lot about you." It wasn't true and Kellan regretted saying it immediately. He extended his hand and Yolanda's father accepted it.

"Kellan is it?"

"Yes," Kellan nodded his head.

"There's not much work here," Yolanda's father said. "This isn't like the city.

"Kellan's not from the city," said Yolanda, "he's from a little village in the west."

"I see. My name's Noah," he said. "How long do you intend to stay?"

"I'm not sure," admitted Kellan, looking at Yolanda, "I hadn't made any definite plans."

"There's a room here for a while if you want it," said Noah, "Yolanda can make the bed up for you."

"Thank you," Kellan smiled, "I appreciate it."

Noah looked at the pots on the stove, "What's this you're making?"

Yolanda lifted one of the lids and clouds of steam rose to the ceiling, "Nothing special, I thought it would be nice to cook you a hot meal."

Noah nodded, "I need to wash up, I'll be half an hour or so." With that he left them and Yolanda gave Kellan a reassuring smile. They sat back at the table and she reached across to him and held his hand. "It'll be alright, thank you for bringing me home."

Kellan was glad to be alone with her and they chatted as they waited. Eventually Noah returned and Yolanda laid the table. Before they ate Noah folded his hands and said grace. As he finished speaking he caught Kellan making the sign of the cross. "Are you a church going man?" Noah asked.

"I intend to be," said Kellan.

"What does that mean?"

"I didn't used to go, but things have changed for me." Kellan found it hard to explain. "I have faith in God." These last words sounded uncomfortably pious and Kellan knew it.

"This is a God-fearing village Kellan; I hope you'll fit in with us."

"I would like to," Kellan said honestly.

Conversation became a little stilted and they ate their food quickly.

"That was good," Kellan said to Yolanda, "I didn't realise you're such a good cook."

"She's some way to go yet before she's as good as her mother was," said Noah. Yolanda smiled at her father and stood to collect the dishes. "So are you planning on staying or is this just a visit?" Noah said.

"I'd like to stay," said Yolanda.

"The city not as exciting as you hoped then?"

"I didn't go looking for excitement It just wasn't for me," she admitted, "I knew that straight away."

"I told you so before you went, but you wouldn't listen."

"What was I supposed to do father? I didn't feel I had any other options."

"Excuse me for saying this Kellan, but there were plenty of men who'd have married you Yolanda. And they'd have given me a decent amount for the privilege too. Running off to the city cost me deep in the purse and there were plenty of folk around here who thought I'd driven you away. How do you think it made me look?"

"I'm sorry for that," said Yolanda, "but you know that's not true. And I could never have married one of those men you had lined up; you want me to love my husband don't you?"

"Love!" Noah laughed with contempt. "We're not talking romance, this is real life. They were decent men, every one of them would have provided for you. They all had a little money behind them."

Kellan felt the last comment was aimed at him but he knew he had nothing to offer that would reassure a father that he could provide for his daughter. Yolanda understood it too.

"How can you reduce me to that?" She spoke in an angry but controlled voice. "I'm not marrying someone because of the number of pigs they have in their yard. Maybe we have different ideas about marriage."

"What do you know about marriage?" Noah said. "You're barely more than a kid. You don't know anything about what it takes to make a marriage work. All that lovey dovey rubbish doesn't last long, and then what have you got?" He reached into his shirt pocket and pulled out a tobacco pouch. As he rolled himself a cigarette he said "I'm sorry Kellan, I don't mean to offend you. I don't know you, there's nothing personal in what I'm saying. I just want what's best for her. She left without my permission and now she turns up with you. What am I supposed to think?"

Before Kellan could say anything Yolanda said "You didn't give me permission to go but you didn't make me want to stay."

"I don't know what you mean Yolanda, what are you saying? What did I ever do wrong?"

"You just wanted me to replace mother in the kitchen, I'd done that for too long. And then when I'd reached an age you wanted to make some money. How was I supposed to feel? I missed her too."

"I never wanted you to replace your mother, that's not true. How could you anyway? But I was working, was it wrong to expect you to help? I thought it was better for you to be busy; I was trying to do the right thing. I didn't do any of it from greed; I always wanted what was best for you."

They fell silent and Noah concentrated on his cigarette. After a moment he turned to Kellan and said "I can invite the minister round for a meal tomorrow."

"We haven't discussed anything like that," said Kellan.

Noah laughed, "I didn't mean to arrange a wedding." He stubbed out the remains of his cigarette, still laughing. "I just thought it would be a chance to find out where you stand on a few things."

"You're not quizzing him over dinner," said Yolanda.

"Calm down," Noah assured her, "I'm not suggesting anything of the sort." He turned to Kellan again, "We take our religion very seriously here. This is a village of good people and if you're going to stay you need to know what's expected. The minister's a decent man, he'll make everything clear."

Noah got to his feet, "I'm going to read. Thank you for the dinner Yolanda, good to meet you Kellan."

When they were alone Yolanda moved to stand by Kellan's side, she put her arms around his neck and pulled his head into her stomach. "I'm sorry," she said, "don't let him worry you."

"It's fine," Kellan said, "I can understand where he's coming from. He doesn't know me, I could be anyone." He reached his arms around her and they stayed like this for a few moments.

"I'll make your bed up later," she said, "I need to wash the pots." She collected the last of the plates from the table and as she attended to them Kellan allowed his thoughts to wander. Eventually he caught himself day dreaming and said "I need to read a little too."

"Go ahead, I won't interrupt you," she said.

Kellan unfolded Elder Ephraim's writings and tried to focus. But he was too affected by the evening's conversation and had to reread a few of the lines in order to take them in. He felt unsettled and his mind was racing. He gave up on the words and watched Yolanda from behind. His desire for her was overpowering but this time he felt there was no sin: he accepted the possibility that he loved her.

Chapter 28

Yolanda took great pleasure in showing off the village to Kellan. She introduced him to various people and recounted stories from her life as the memories came back to her. He enjoyed seeing this other side to her and her happiness relaxed him. He noticed a great pride amongst the villagers for their home, something Yolanda shared in. Often they would tell him what good people lived there and he began to suspect that this really was the end of his journey.

Yolanda found him a number of small jobs around the house and yard and Kellan was relieved to have something to contribute, hoping that it would please her father when he came home. At lunch time they walked out to a flat meadow and ate a simple meal that she had prepared for them. There was a cold breeze and Yolanda pressed herself against him as closely as she could. When they had finished eating they chatted casually, looking out over the field and watching the birds in the trees.

Kellan felt his desire for her like never before and kissed her. It was a gesture full of intent and she pulled away. As she did so he realised how he must have seemed to her and pulled back. "I'm sorry, I forgot myself."

"No, you mustn't apologise, that's not why I stopped you." She grew serious and looked away from him.

"What is it?" Kellan asked. "Have I done something wrong?"

"No, nothing, it's something else. There's something I need to tell you."

"What is it Yolanda?"

As she looked at him he saw her eyes filling with tears. "I'm so sorry Kellan. There's something you have to know."

"Just say it Yolanda, don't upset yourself."

"You remember back in the city, when I told you about the merchant I worked for."

"The one who tried to force you into selling yourself?" Kellan said.

"Yes, well there's more to the story. I was frightened when I first got there; he was kind enough to give me work and lodgings. One thing led to another and..." Her voice trailed away.

"What is it Yolanda, please tell me."

"I slept with him Kellan, it was stupid and I regret it, I wanted to tell you before but I couldn't bring myself to."

She stared ahead of them, waiting for his response.

"I don't care Yolanda; I can see how you feel about it. Do you think my past is spotless?"

She turned to look at him and with gratitude said "Thank you Kellan, you don't now how much I needed to tell you. I didn't know how you'd react." She embraced him and kissed his face.

"I'm sorry you had to go through that, how could I hold it against you?"

"I thought his feelings were real," she said. "But once it started he started talking about making money. I was so ashamed Kellan, the things he said to me made me feel worthless. I thought he was right, I slept with him and felt ashamed and when he called me those names I couldn't think of a reason to deny them. It wasn't until I met you in the prison that I thought I could ever think of myself in any other way."

"It's gone now," he whispered. "Let it go, we mustn't hold on to any of it."

"Thank you for forgiving me Kellan."

"I have nothing to forgive. You didn't know me then, and besides, like I said, my past is so full of shame that I don't have the right to judge anyone."

"Were there many women in your past?"

"No, not many. I didn't mean that."

"What then Kellan? Tell me."

He took a deep breath, like a man about to dive from a high board. "I ran away when my village was attacked by bandits."

"What else could you have done? If you hadn't run you'd be dead. I don't understand what you think you've done wrong."

"I was a coward Yolanda, I thought only of my own safety. I didn't just run away for safety, I didn't even consider trying to help anyone, I only cared about me."

She squeezed him tight, "I don't think that's who you are now. I don't believe you would ever leave me like that."

244

As she said this Kellan believed it too. There was no part of him that could imagine abandoning her to anything, regardless of the consequences to him. He kissed her hair in gratitude.

They sat in the meadow until the cold had penetrated their clothing. Yolanda wanted to start cooking the evening meal and so they walked back to the village, Kellan's arm around her shoulders. Back at the house she refused his offer of help and so he left her in the kitchen and went up to his room. He sat on the bed and laid Elder Ephraim's writings across his lap. The pages now were like the finest silk, Kellan admired the workmanship in the stitching and lifted it to his lips and kissed it. His kiss was not for the beauty of an object, but for what it represented to him. He opened to the page he had marked and began to read.

The devil's temptations are like voices calling out to us in the night, pleading with us to join them in revelry and sin. The wise man shuts his doors so that he cannot hear them, but the fool calls back to answer them.

Kellan stretched out on the bed and tried to understand what this meant but his thoughts kept returning to Yolanda. He gave up on the text and began to think through all that he and Yolanda had talked about during the day. The idea of settling in the village was appealing to him and he weighed up different options about work. He decided he would ask if anyone needed a farm hand but failing that he would approach the baker and see if there was a vacancy. But no matter what happened he had the growing realisation that as long as they were together he could cope with anything.

It was growing dark by the time Noah returned from work. Kellan heard their brief conversation in the kitchen and then the sound of splashing water as Noah washed himself. Kellan went down to Yolanda and found her stirring something on the stove.

"Smells good," he said.

"It will be another hour. The minister's coming."

Kellan was unsure how to react and forced a smile.

"Don't worry," she said, "it's not a test."

Kellan laughed, "I'm not sure I'd pass if it was. I didn't have much time for church before I met Father Paisios."

"Just be yourself. We've got nothing to prove. It's just father wanting to show there's nothing odd going on. Once the minister meets you he'll see what a good man you are and father will relax. You know what it can be like in a small town. Tongues start wagging if you're not careful. Father just wants to make sure no one gets any silly ideas."

Kellan wasn't encouraged by anything she said but managed to conceal his feelings. He sat down at the table and started counting down the minutes. He tried to pray but his thoughts were too distracted.

It was less than an hour later when they heard Noah greeting the minister at the door. The visitor's voice was a deep baritone that seemed to reverberate through the house. Kellan threw

Yolanda a quick look and then stood to greet their guest. The minister was a large man in every way, tall and barrel chested. He strode in confidently dressed in a smart suit and smelling of expensive cologne.

He shook hands with Kellan and continued to hold his hand after the greeting. "I'm pleased to meet you Kellan; I hope you've been made to feel welcome in our town."

"Yes," said Kellan, "everyone's been very friendly."

"That's good, and no less than I would expect. We are commanded to welcome the widow and the stranger, the people here are well aware of their Christian duty."

Noah greeted Kellan and said "There may be work at one of the farms if they think you're up to it. I spoke to them today."

"Thank you Noah, I appreciate that."

"This is Reverend Moses," said Noah.

Kellan felt he was the centre of attention and was relieved when the minister addressed Yolanda. "How have you been since we last saw you?"

"Good, thank you Reverend."

"I hope you have been good Yolanda, the devil stalks the streets of that city like a roaring lion."

"We know only too well," Yolanda agreed. "We couldn't get away quick enough."

"How long were you living there Kellan?" The minister pulled out a chair as he spoke and squeezed his large frame behind the table.

"A few weeks," said Kellan.

"Did you attend the church there?"

"No," said Kellan, "they charge entry and I hadn't earned enough in the short time I was there."

"You hear that Noah," the minister said, "charging people to pray to their God. What kind of people are they? They have veered from the path of truth. They are so far from it that I would be wary of calling them Christian."

Noah and Kellan took their seats while Yolanda busied herself with the food. The minister was holding court and Kellan could see he was used to having it this way.

"We have struggled hard to build a Christian community here Kellan; the church is at the centre of our lives. We have achieved so much in very little time: the Lord has rewarded us for our labours. When I first arrived there was a terrible division in the community, it threatened the good order of the whole village. But we managed to cast out the voices of disorder; our life here has been strengthened and blessed because we have kept to the true path. For a while there were men here who thought as the city church thinks, they polluted the hearts and minds of many people. But I must say, with not a little humility, that I was able to shepherd my flock away from these temptations into the Promised Land we now enjoy."

"Kellan is a devout man," Yolanda said. "He reads holy words all the time." Kellan regretted her saying this, he knew it would renew the sense of being inspected he had had since Reverend Moses arrived.

"What kind of writings are these?" Moses asked him.

"They're just a collection of reflections, nothing more really."

"Come on Kellan," said Yolanda. "They mean far more to you than that."

"I'd very much like to see them," said Reverend Moses.

"I'll get them," said Yolanda, but Kellan stood to stop her.

"No, leave them Yolanda, they're very personal. I don't think there's anything that would interest him."

"Nonsense Kellan," said Reverend Moses, "let's see them girl."

Yolanda pushed past Kellan went up to his room to find them while the minister continued with his speech. "I see people working hard to live good lives everywhere I go in our community. If there is one fruit sweeter than any other in the Christian life it is good character and moral fortitude."

"Sweeter than prayer?" Kellan asked.

"What good is prayer if a man lives a sinful life?" Moses said.

"Aren't we all sinners Reverend?" Kellan regretted his words immediately.

"It is true we haven't yet reached the perfection of our Lord but I don't think you'll find many examples of sin in this village. Believe me Kellan, I would know if there were any."

"A good man once told me that it is important to always be aware of our sin, to stay focussed on it so that we don't allow ourselves to fall into pride," said Kellan.

"And the good book tells me that our Lord said we shouldn't hide our light but let it shine for all to see. If we are living the way God wants us to we should let everyone know about it. We become an encouragement to our neighbour and the works of God are manifest for all to see." Moses' voice was beginning to boom, his enthusiasm for his message was only equalled by his capacity to declare it.

"My friend told me to never imagine myself as doing anything good but always see myself in God's debt." Kellan was becoming nervous and it took great effort to speak the words.

"Why would a Christian want to grovel in their sins like that? Those of us who have been saved know we are forgiven. Don't you believe God forgives?" There was now a tone of accusation in the Reverend's voice and Kellan knew he shouldn't say too much.

"The more I am aware of my sins, the more I have to thank God for," said Kellan.

Before Moses could respond Yolanda returned with Elder Ephraim's writings. She smiled as she laid them before the minister, oblivious to Kellan's concern.

"These old things?" Moses said. "I can barely make out the words." He took out his reading glasses and peered into the pages like a doctor searching for a patient's cause of death. "What on earth is this?" He prodded the page with the tip of his finger and turned to Noah. "Read that," he said.

Noah stared at the writing and shook his head but said nothing.

"Why would any Christian call someone the Mother of God? I've rarely heard such blasphemy. God has no mother Kellan, how could the eternal God need a mother?"

Kellan cleared his throat. "Christ was God come to earth. He was born of a woman like every one of us. The Mother of God truly gave birth to God, how else could He become man?"

"I don't need lecturing on the incarnation of our Lord!" Said Moses, "but it is too much to use such terms. And see here, it talks of praying to her. How can we pray to anyone but God? This is blasphemy!" He pushed the writings away from him across the table for dramatic effect.

"We pray to the saints to ask for their prayers. They don't do anything except in the power of God. Just as we ask each other to pray for us, so we ask the saints to remember us before God. We aren't praying to them as gods." Kellan had never expressed the ideas outwardly before and his discomfort was continuing to grow.

"No Kellan, we need no intermediary, we all have access to the scriptures, none of us need someone to speak on our behalf." Moses tapped his finger on the table with the rhythm of his words and his neck was beginning to redden.

"Does no one ever ask you to pray for them Reverend?" Kellan's voice was suddenly calm and controlled.

"That's very different, I am a living man. We are instructed in the scriptures not to converse with the dead. It is in black and white, there can be no exceptions."

"When we pray to the saints we do not converse with the dead, for in Christ all are alive. The saints live on, death has been overcome." Kellan looked around the room for agreement but Noah looked down at the ground and Yolanda looked back at him with a mixture of concern and confusion.

"On the day of judgement, yes," said Reverend Moses. "But until then the dead sleep and await their fate."

"Didn't Christ promise the thief on the cross that he would be in paradise that very day?" Kellan reached across the table and took back Elder Ephraim's writings. "I'm sorry to disagree with you Reverend Moses, but this is what I have been shown and this is what I believe."

Reverend Moses looked thoughtfully at him and then with a new calmness in his voice said "You must come to church on Sunday. All these words around a dinner table are one thing, but when we join our voices in praise none of these things matter. Will you join us Kellan?"

"Yes, I'd like that," he said. "I didn't mean to create an argument."

"Let's forget such things," said Reverend Moses. "I smell a good meal on the stove and we mustn't give ourselves indigestion with such conversation."

Yolanda looked relieved at this but for the rest of the evening Kellan said very little. He wasn't confident enough in his understanding of these matters to be sure he was right but something told him that the man before him had very little in common with the faith he had witnessed in the forest at Father Paisios' cell.

At the end of the evening Reverend Moses thanked everyone for a good evening and Noah accompanied him to the door. They stood there for some time and Kellan sensed that he was at least partly the subject of their conversation as he heard the muffled voices coming through to the kitchen. Once Noah returned Kellan made his excuses and went up to his room. He lay in the dark attempting to pray, but all the time sensed a heavy presence pressing down on him. His feelings for Yolanda created a longing in him for everything to be right, but he perceived a threat that was impossible to name.

Chapter 29

The following day Kellan met with one of the local farmers and was given work. He was employed to do general labouring, much like he had done at home, but now that he felt he was working for both he and Yolanda he felt a greater enthusiasm for the tasks. He even found the work gave him time to pray while he completed the physical labour and he sensed that his life was finally recovering some kind of normality. At dinner Yolanda made a point of asking him about his day in front of her father and Noah's acceptance of him seemed to be growing.

No one in the village worked on Saturday afternoons and Yolanda took Kellan for a long walk in the nearby hills. From there they looked out over the village and Kellan was impressed with the good order of the fields. They strolled back holding hands and Kellan began to feel a happiness he had never known before. Her willingness to accept his past gave him a feeling of openness, a sense that he no longer had a secret to conceal from the world.

On Sunday morning Noah leant Kellan some smarter clothes and the three of them followed the sound of bells to church. As they got closer they met others in dark suits and polite greetings were exchanged. The church was a large wooden structure that looked plain but imposing. As they entered Kellan noticed the clean white walls and polished floor which communicated how important this place was to the parishioners.

Noah took his seat on a long wooden pew and Yolanda and Kellan followed behind. The church was filling quickly and Kellan could sense the curiosity his presence was stirring. A middle-aged woman stopped beside their pew and greeted Noah.

"Hello Ruth," he said.

"Hello Noah, good to see you back Yolanda." Her eyes settled on Kellan. Yolanda introduced him and the woman nodded but said nothing.

Kellan began to look around and realised that there were no images of any kind, not even in the glass windows. At the far end of the church was a simple wooden cross but this was dwarfed by a large pulpit carved in dark, ornate wood. The pulpit's presence dominated the room and even while it was empty everyone stared ahead towards it in expectation.

To some unseen signal the congregation stood and a pipe organ began to play. The notes were dreary and solemn and as they drifted over the heads of the worshippers Reverend Moses made his entrance. He processed solemnly down the centre isle his head bowed and his hands pressed together at his chest in front of him. He wore a long black cassock and a white stole around his neck. As he reached the pulpit he slowly ascended the steps and took his place above the congregation. Only now did he seem to notice that anyone else was in the room as he allowed his gaze to move across the faces before him, checking to see that all were present. A few late-comers were still finding their seats and his gaze rested on them as they rushed to their places. The music ended and everyone remained standing as he recited the first prayer in a loud and monotone voice asking God to bless their gathering. It was greeted with a unanimous "Amen" and everyone joined in with the singing of the first hymn the words of which they all knew.

Kellan took the opportunity to turn and look around at the rest of the church and saw that above the door were written the Ten Commandments in large black lettering. The script gave them a threatening appearance and as Kellan turned back to face the pulpit he found the Reverend's stare fixed on him. So intense was the look in his eyes that Kellan looked away, unsure of the intention behind them.

The hymn ended and everyone took their seat. Reverend Moses opened the largest Bible Kellan had ever seen and in the familiar booming voice the congregation listened to the words of the Old Testament condemning various activities. Kellan tried to focus on the reading but the dramatic delivery made it impossible and he began to wish for the end of the service. After a few more hymns, readings and prayers Reverend Moses began his sermon. He took for his theme the need for faith above all things and it was clear to all that here was a man who had had a long education. He connected different verses and teachings in such a complicated and thorough way that no one could have failed to have been impressed. Around him

Kellan noticed people nodding their heads in agreement, they were transfixed by the Reverend's performance, but there was something more beyond this. Despite the emptiness of the service itself, where God was talked about at great length but rarely addressed directly, Kellan recognised that the people around him were genuinely devout; in their faces he could see a longing for something, a genuine desire for God. But Kellan struggled to connect what he saw in the people with what their minister was delivering and knew that they deserved more. The constraints of the service imposed a rigidity on them, they had squeezed themselves into a formality that had an outward appearance of solemnity but lacked any real spiritual content. As the words and music flowed over him Kellan knew that it was bringing him no closer to God, and now, as the sermon dragged on Reverend Moses was merely putting on a show to convince his listeners of how knowledgeable he was.

Kellan looked along the pew and saw Noah sitting stiffly to attention, his expressionless face looking almost inhuman like some carving in stone. Yolanda was making the effort to assume the same pose but every so often she glanced over at Kellan to check his reactions. It brought Kellan a sense of confusion. The yearning for God that Father Paisios had ignited within him had nothing n common with what was happening around him. He couldn't understand how the two experiences could be so different and his desire to please Yolanda and her father only made the confusion more intense. He struggled to contain his feelings and told himself to conceal whatever he felt. He needed time to think through what all this might mean and adopted a look every bit as blank as Noah's.

Finally the service came to an end with yet another dreary hymn that suffocated the last embers of joy that might have glowed in anyone's chest. The congregation began to file out past the Reverend at the door. Each shook his hand and exchanged a few quick words, and as Kellan approached he could see how most of the congregation were in awe of him. Noah extended his hand to Reverend Moses, "Thank you for another excellent sermon," he said.

The Reverend smiled at the compliment, "It is an honour to preach the Lord's message." He looked at Kellan, "How are you?"

"Good, thank you," said Kellan.

"What do you think of our church Kellan?"

"It's a beautiful building."

"Yes, the Lord has rewarded us for our labour. But what about the service Kellan, how did you get on with our worship?"

Kellan couldn't find the words to hide his feelings; he stammered and mumbled something incoherent.

"What was that?" Reverend Moses said.

"I...I haven't experienced worship like that before." Kellan answered.

"What was so different?" The Reverend fixed his whole attention on Kellan just as he had from the pulpit.

"I'm not sure," said Kellan, "I don't know how to put it into words."

Reverend Moses grew pensive; he continued to stare at Kellan for a moment and then turned back to Noah. "We must meet again soon," he said.

With that the Reverend turned his attention to the flattery of the next group of parishioners and Kellan and the others walked away. Noah was silent and Yolanda tried to relieve the tension. "I'll cook us a good meal tonight," she said, slipping her arm through Kellan's. Neither man responded and they headed home. Noah disappeared into his room and Yolanda and Kellan took their seats at the table while they waited for the water to boil for their tea.

"What was wrong at church?" She asked.

He paused before answering, "I'm not sure, something just didn't feel right."

"What do you mean Kellan? Didn't you enjoy it?"

"No, I felt uneasy; I didn't feel like I belonged there."

"You'll get used to everyone," she said. "It's not easy meeting so many new people all at once."

"No, it's not that, it wasn't the people. It was the service; I couldn't connect it with anything I know about God."

"What does that mean?" Yolanda's voice was full of concern.

"I'm not sure; I just didn't feel like we were praying." He looked at her for her reaction and could see how uneasy his words were making her feel.

"But that's ridiculous," she said. "You heard Reverend Moses, there were lots of prayers."

"I heard him speaking, and I heard him saying things about how we should live, but was that it? Were you able to pray when he was talking?"

"He said the words for us," said Yolanda. "I listened to him and agreed with him. What more did you expect?"

"But did you feel God with you?"

"What do you mean?" Yolanda was becoming annoyed. "How could you expect the Reverend to conjure up those kinds of feelings? I'm not sure what you think we were doing."

"I didn't expect him to conjure anything up. But when I prayed with Father Paisios I could feel him praying for me. I could feel myself being drawn closer to God, and I knew God was there. Not just a thought of God or a belief in God. I could feel Him with us. And ever since then I've had moments like that. But not in your church, it didn't do anything like that."

"We learned so much from his sermon," she said. "We were reminded not to sin and the Reverend told us how to be better Christians. Isn't that enough Kellan? It's enough for everyone else here."

"That's just because they haven't experienced what real worship can be like."

"That's just so arrogant Kellan. Who are you to judge what these people have or have not experienced with God?"

"I know, I'm sorry." Kellan shook his head. "I have no right to make judgements about them; I could see they were genuine. I'm not criticising them, I promise Yolanda. But how could they be satisfied with that service? How could they think that that's all there is to it?"

The water was boiling and Yolanda prepared the cups. She turned her back to him and he knew he had upset her. "I need to go for a walk," he said. "I need to think abut it all. I'm sorry if I've upset you."

They drank their tea and before leaving he squeezed her hand to which she gave a weak smile. He pulled on one of Noah's coats and left the house. He walked up to the edge of the village and stood looking out across one of the fields he had been working in two days before. As he stood there Noah came up behind him, "Mind if I join you?"

"Oh hello, no of course."

"Yolanda spoke to me about how you felt in church."

Kellan's heart sank as he heard this, he didn't feel clear in his own mind about what he was feeling and he certainly wasn't ready to explain himself to her father.

"I'm concerned about it Kellan, I won't pretend otherwise."

"I'm sorry Noah, I'm not trying to cause problems."

"That may well be, but Yolanda is confused and I'm not happy about that."

"I didn't want to upset her Noah; I need to sort my thinking out. I just need a little time."

"She's had a difficult time through the years Kellan. I know I haven't been the greatest father in the world. I don't know what she's told you about me, but I always wanted the best for her."

"She's only ever spoken well of you," Kellan said honestly.

"That's good to know, but I've always tried to bring her up as a good Christian. When her mother died I was left with everything to do. Reverend Moses has been a great help through the years, I have a lot to be grateful to that man for." He turned to face Kellan and his voice grew quieter. "If I think you're upsetting things for us, I can't have you staying any longer. That goes for the whole village. If you cause problems it's best if you go. I'm not throwing you out Kellan, but you need to understand the way things are. Before Reverend Moses calmed things down here it was a terrible time. We had two churches in the village and the whole community was divided."

"What happened to the other church?" Kellan said.

"It's gone." Noah narrowed his lips, "it burned down."

It was clear to Kellan what this meant and it didn't surprise him. "What about the people who worshipped there?"

"Some of them left, some of them joined us. A few..." His voice trailed off. He gave Kellan a look of warning, "Don't rock the boat."

Kellan wasn't sure if there was meant to be a threat or a warning in Noah's words, but as the older man walked away Kellan knew with absolute certainty that this was not the place Father Paisios had spoken of. But knowing that he couldn't stay made him realise how much he loved Yolanda. It was unbearable to imagine leaving her, and he began to contemplate what he should do. He stood praying as the evening sun was sinking: all he knew now with any certainty was that he had to talk to her.

Chapter 30

Back at the house Yolanda was sitting in the small living room beside the fire. The only light came from the flames which danced in the grate and on the walls around her the moving shadows gave life to the stillness of the scene. She said nothing as Kellan entered and took off the coat he had borrowed. He sat on the other side of the fire and could see she had been crying.

"Are you alright?" He asked.

She glanced at him and then looked back into the flames. "I don't know Kellan."

"Don't worry, we can find a way through this." He reached over and held her hand and felt her fingers curling around his.

"Father is serious; don't think this can be brushed aside."

"I don't Yolanda; I understand how important this is to him. It's important to me too."

"I know it is, I'm sorry." Her hand tightened around his and she forced a smile. "I just don't want anything to mess things up for us. Kellan, I love you."

He slipped from his chair and knelt down before her. "I love you Yolanda, I won't let anything get in the way."

She shook her head. "No, I know you feel like that, but it's not that simple."

"What do you mean?"

"It's not just about us Kellan. No matter how much we love each other, we have to think of other people."

"I know, I don't want to be selfish. But I do love you, and that's the most important thing to me right now."

"But I love my father too, and I love the people here." She took both of his hands in hers. "We're not children Kellan; we can't just do as we please."

"I know, I don't want to upset anyone. But if we can't be together here we could go somewhere else. There are other villages."

"I don't know what to think Kellan. When I went to the city it hurt my father, I can't do that to him again. He hasn't got anyone else but me. He pretends to be strong but he needs me." Tears began to tumble down her cheeks. "I won't run away again."

Kellan didn't know what to say. He admired her care for her father and recognised his own desire to act selfishly. "We don't have to make a decision now, let's give it a little time."

She wiped her eyes, "There isn't time."

"What do you mean? Has your father said something?"

"Yes, he's worried about me and you. He came back earlier and told me he'd spoken to you. Some of the church elders are afraid of what you might do to the village."

"I'm not going to do anything to the village! What have they got to be afraid of?"

"Your beliefs, your reaction to Reverend Moses. Father says it sounds like the heretics who used to live here. They're afraid that you'll start all those troubles up again."

"I promise Yolanda, I won't stir anything up. I won't breathe a word about anything to anyone. There's nothing to fear."

"Father says you've already started having an influence on me, so who knows where it will end?"

"I haven't done anything to change your views Yolanda. What do they think I've said?"

"It's those writings you brought into the village. Reverend Moses says they're the real threat."

"That's nonsense. You've read some of them. Do you think like this?"

"No Kellan, I found them full of grace, they're beautiful words. But Reverend Moses thinks differently. I don't run the village, it doesn't matter what I think."

"Then come away with me Yolanda, we don't have to go far. If I'm not fit for this place come with me."

"I told you why I can't. Please don't put pressure on me." She let go of Kellan's hands and wiped her face again. "I don't know how we can resolve this Kellan; I don't know what to do."

"We must pray Yolanda, will you pray with me now?"

She nodded and they bowed their heads. Kellan asked the Mother of God to intercede for them and they sensed God's presence with them. As Kellan spoke they became aware of another presence and looking up they found Noah standing in the doorway listening.

"You persist in this despite what I said to you?" His voice was controlled but angry.

"We were just praying father, please don't think anything of it."

"I heard what he said, praying to his saints, I made it clear how we feel. And still he does this in my house. That's it Kellan, I can't have you living here any longer. Tomorrow you'll leave."

Yolanda began to cry as Noah left them and went to his room. Kellan put his arms around her but she couldn't be comforted. "Will you come with me Yolanda?" He whispered.

"I don't know," she lifted her head and looked at him, "I want to, I love you, but I don't know what to do."

"Okay, don't force yourself to make a decision now. Get a night's sleep, pray about it Yolanda. Ask the Mother of God to pray for you, and trust in God. If you do this then God will help you to see what you should do. Will you do that?"

"Yes," she nodded. "I'm sorry Kellan; I didn't want any of this."

"I know, it's alright. We'll talk in the morning. I'll pray for you, we must trust in God."

They embraced once more and he stood to leave. "I do love you Yolanda, please remember that." She smiled back at him and watched him leave. She turned back to the fire and with the heat of the flames bathing her face she closed her eyes and began to pray.

Kellan sat on his bed and tried to clear his head. He tried to plan how he should react to whatever decision Yolanda made but the thought of leaving her was stirring too many emotions. His anxiety was creating a tension that he could feel physically in his chest and stomach and he knew that if he allowed his feelings to control his actions he risked doing or saying something that might convince Yolanda to stay. He wanted to remain honest and open with her but he knew that he was prepared to do or say anything to persuade her to come with him.

He tried to pray but his thoughts kept returning to her and so he reached for Elder Ephraim's writings and turned to the last page.

Do not be afraid to release your grip on the things of this world for the wise man knows that heaven's joys are eternal. The sufferings we patiently endure in this life build a crown in the next. We must endure all things knowing that God permits them for the good of our soul. The One who loves us more than we love ourselves allows evil to befall us so that we may conquer the enemy who hates us. Accept all things as though they were sent by God and you will know peace if you truly believe that God loves you and in His infinite wisdom arranges all things to enable you to find salvation. God sends us every opportunity to become heirs to His kingdom, if only we would raise our desires from the earth.

Kellan felt a peace as he read and closed his eyes to pray. He understood that he was in God's care and gave himself to what ever would be God's will. He lay back on the bed still holding the writings to his chest and eventually he fell to sleep.

A hand smothered his mouth and as Kellan's eyes flashed open he could make out figures in the darkness around his bed. But before his eyes could adjust a sack was pulled over his head and tied around his neck. He could feel hands gripping his arms and legs and he was rolled over onto his stomach. His hands were tied behind his back and he was lifted free of the bed and carried face down from the room. A hand continued to press tightly from outside the sack over his mouth as he was taken from the house.

He was carried some distance until without warning he was dropped to the floor, his face hit the ground and he let out a cry of pain. There were no voices but Kellan sensed a large number of men from the way they so easily tossed him around. He felt them take his arms and he was pulled upright as he scrambled to find his footing. His wrists were tied and the nightshirt ripped from his back. There was a pause in the activity and he strained to hear who was there.

"Who are you?" His question went unanswered, "Please, what are you doing?"

Even before his brain could register the sound of leather moving through the air he felt the lash of a whip cutting into his back. The shock of the sting drove the air from his lungs and he gasped and moaned simultaneously. He was struck a second time and the intense pain burned across his body, forcing another involuntary cry from him. Each time the pain was as severe as the first strike and he pulled hard against the ropes around his wrists as he braced himself against it. The next lash caused his legs to buckle and as he dropped his body's weight pulled hard on the ropes which cut into his flesh.

"Please," he could barely speak. "No more, I'll go."

Two more strikes of the whip left him close to collapse, his back now felt like a single slab of pain, each wound inseparable from any other. The wounds had cut deep and blood now ran down his legs.

As he gasped for breath the hood was pulled from his head and a hand grabbed a fist of his hair. His head was pulled back and he saw Reverend Moses before him.

"Look what you've done," the Reverend's deep voice sounded almost concerned. "Why couldn't you listen? No one wants this Kellan; God knows I tried to avoid it. But you wouldn't listen. We can't have you destroying what we have created here; you don't have the right to take our peace from us."

"Please," Kellan gasped, "I'll go."

"And what about poor Yolanda? You've filled her head with your lies. You've spread your corruption in just a few days, we can't let this continue. I reached out to you Kellan; I gave you the chance to repent. I prayed for you, and I will go on praying for you, but you've given us no choice."

"You don't have to do this, I'll go," Kellan pleaded.

"Don't you think I care about you too?" The Reverend's face leaned into Kellan's. "What kind of minister would I be if I allowed you to wander off in this state? No, it's my duty to pull you from the devil's snare. I take no pleasure from this, but my joy will overflow to know I have saved you from the fire of hell. Tell me you reject the things you have been saying, say it now and save yourself."

"I can't, I don't know what you want me to say." Kellan struggled to form the words.

"Liar!" The Reverend's voice rose in anger. "Reject this evil desire to talk to the dead, the saints you speak to, they have no place in the Bible. Repent of this now and save yourself. Say it Kellan, for the good of your soul."

Kellan closed his eyes; there was nothing he could say. He knew he could not betray all that he had come to believe, any more than he could deny his love for Yolanda. He looked past his accuser and saw the first hints of sunrise across the sky, the night was nearly over.

As Reverend Moses let go of his hair Kellan's head flopped forwards. The Reverend walked away and Kellan could hear him giving instructions. From the trees above them came the calls of many crows, their voices sounded like mocking laughter. Kellan managed to lift his head and saw one of the men from the village throwing a rope over a high tree branch. As he did so the crows took to the air, their black shapes like rags in the wind. At the end of the rope was a loop and Kellan knew it was intended for his neck. He clenched his eyes tight and began to pray. He called out Father Paisios' name and then fell silent. He remembered the fear when he had run from his village and understood he should have given his life that day. And now in the last moments of his life on earth he grasped what the old monk in the woods had been telling him. His destination was not to be found in the villages of men, it was a place beyond this world. As a deep peace filled him the pain in his back subsided and he longed for nothing but to be with God.

The ropes at his wrists were untied and his hands pulled behind his back. One of the men stood in front of him holding him up and then dragged him to the tree. Kellan felt the rough rope slide over his head and the voice of Reverend Moses imploring him to deny his heresy. Kellan opened his eyes one last time and saw the hate and fury in the faces of the world he was leaving. He looked into the eyes of the men before him and recognised the wounds of life that had brought them to such action and with a genuine compassion prayed for them.

Two of the men began pulling the other end of the rope which tightened around Kellan's throat and lifted him from his feet. The men who had been supporting him let go and his body weight pulled down through the muscle and bone of his neck. But Kellan had already died to any claim they could make on him, and as his body choked his victory was complete as he entered the city built in eternity.

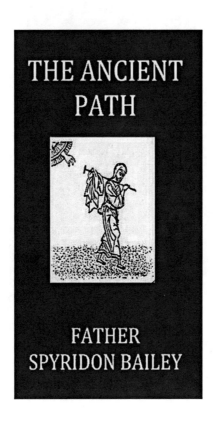

THE ANCIENT PATH

FATHER
SPYRIDON BAILEY

The Ancient Path is a collection of reflections based on quotations from the Fathers of the Orthodox Church. It is available from Amazon and Amazon Kindle.

JOURNEY TO MOUNT ATHOS

FATHER SPYRIDON BAILEY

Journey To Mount Athos describes Father Spyridon's encounters with monks and hermits during his pilgrimage to the Holy Mountain.

Fire On The Lips tells the story of a young couple's encounter with a monk who over the next four decades leads them deeper into the ancient mystical experience of the Orthodox Church.

CPSIA information can be obtained
at www.ICGtesting.com
Printed in the USA
FSOW01n1954230917
39047FS